Erin,

B[?] your adventure!

[signature]

Cauldron
Cooker's
Night

Erin,

Real her[?]

[signature] David Anthony

Dedication

David:
Paul J. Serratoni

Charlie:
Jozlyn, my daughter

Additionally, both writers would like to express a sincere
thank you to Margot Williston for her tireless enthusiasm
and support.

ISBN 0-9728461-0-7

Printed in the U.S.A.

First Printing, July 2003
Fourth Printing, September 2005

Cauldron Cooker's Night
Table of Contents

Fantasy Name Guide
for
Cauldron Cooker's Night

In fantasy books like Knightscares, some character names
will be familiar to you. Some will not. To help you
pronounce the tough ones, here's a handy guide to the
unusual names found in
Knightscares #1: Cauldron Cooker's Night.

Cleogha
Klee - o - guh

griznt
griz - nit

Mephello
Meh - fell - low

Mougi
Moo - gee

Pa Gnobbles
Nah - bulls

Zeila
Zee - luh

Tiller's Field and Surroundings

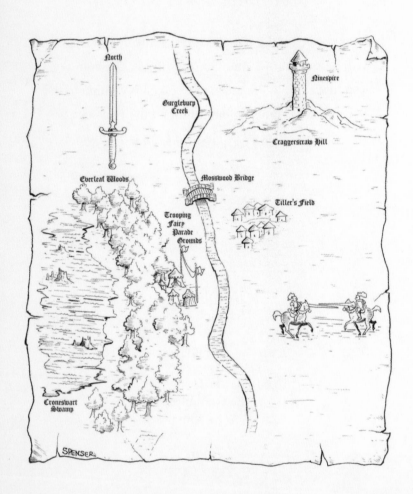

#1:
Cauldron Cooker's Night

David Anthony
and
Charles David

Trouble's Brewing

1

"Jozlyn," I whispered in the dark, "are you scared?" I could hear her in the bed on the other side of the room talking quietly to her pixie doll, Rosie, so I knew she was still awake.

Jozlyn didn't call Rosie a doll. She was too old for dolls. She called Rosie her *friend* and behaved exactly as if Rosie was a real pixie.

"Of *c*-course not, Josh," she replied in a stutter as if I'd surprised her. "But it's all right if you are."

Oh sure, I thought. That was just like Jozlyn. As my older sister, she thought she was smarter, faster, and stronger than I was. Now she acted like she was braver, too. She never quit.

Jozlyn had just turned thirteen. She was a teenager now. Add that to the fact that she was four inches taller than me, and she was almost impossible to live with.

I was eleven, and at that moment Jozlyn really had the upper hand. Until my birthday in three weeks, she was two years older instead of just one.

I decided to try a trick my Dad had taught me. He said that sisters don't always tell the whole truth but their dolls usually do.

"What about Rosie?" I asked, trying to sound casual. "Is she afraid?"

I wanted to ask *What about your little doll?* but didn't think it was the best time to pick a fight. Even though I wouldn't admit it to Jozlyn, I was nervous.

"Hmm," Jozlyn mumbled. She sat up in her bed and I could see her in the dim light coming through our window.

Jozlyn's hair was long and blonde like Mom's. Mine is short and dark like Dad's. Jozlyn wore a white nightgown embroidered with horses in different colors of thread. There were prancing horses, galloping horses, rearing horses, and grazing horses. Jozlyn was crazy about horses.

"Well, maybe a little scared," she admitted, "but not too much. Rosie has magic, don't forget."

Here we go again, I thought, rolling my eyes. *More of how Rosie isn't just a doll.* Jozlyn was always telling people that Rosie had magic like a wizard.

Or a witch.

I shivered under my blanket and hoped Jozlyn didn't

notice. Tonight was Cauldron Cooker's Night, a holiday for witches. That was why we couldn't sleep. We'd already been lying in our beds for a long time trying to fall asleep.

Witches rode their brooms all night long in celebration of the spooky holiday. They shrieked and cackled and kept people awake. Supposedly they also tried to catch children who weren't asleep to throw into a big pot for a midnight snack.

So far, I hadn't heard anything unusual. Just crickets and a dog barking. The normal nighttime sounds.

That could change at any time. A witch named Cleogha lived on the edge of town where she sold herbs, love potions, and charms to ward off trolls. Cleogha's charms must work because I'd never seen a troll, and Tiller's Field, where I lived, was a pretty big town.

My friend Connor claimed he had seen a troll once. But he was always making up stories, so I'm not sure I believed him. He'd said the troll had been fishing from Mosswood Bridge.

"You know, Mom and Dad will be mad if we don't get to sleep," Jozlyn reminded in a know-it-all voice. "We have to be up early to save a seat by the fountain to see the Fairy Troops."

Bossing me around was her way of changing the subject. I could tell she didn't want to talk or think about witches or their cauldrons any more than I did. Not on Cauldron

Cooker's Night, especially.

Tomorrow was the Trooping Fairy Day Parade when all the fairies from Everleaf Woods gathered to celebrate the arrival of summer. They played tiny instruments, sang songs, and put on a parade at the edge of the forest.

All the townsfolk attended the celebration. There were archery competitions, fencing, storytelling, games like unicorn horns, a pie-eating contest, and a big feast in the evening. The mysterious Wizard Ast was even going to come down from his tower to perform some magic tricks.

I really wanted to fall asleep. Nothing was more exciting than Trooping Fairy Day, except maybe my birthday. The sooner I slept, the sooner tomorrow would arrive and the fun would begin.

Not to mention that a witch wouldn't catch me awake and stick me in her pot.

"Why don't you hush and go to sleep yourself? I'm pretty tired," I told Jozlyn as I faked a big yawn. "And I'm not scared one bit."

Jozlyn harrumphed and made a big show of flopping back down on her bed. "Well, I'm not scared, and neither is Rosie."

Even in the dim light, I knew Jozlyn was sticking her tongue out at me. I could feel it. I flopped over on my side, turning my back to her.

After that, I must have slept for a while because when I

opened my eyes next pale moonlight shined in through the window. A strange noise very close by had awakened me.

Whoosh!

The noise came again.

Parent Trap

2

The strange noise came from right outside our window. It sounded like a flock of large bats flapping by at high speed. I didn't see what caused it, but the moonlight flickered as it passed.

I held my breath and didn't move. The noise was Witch Cleogha on her broom, I just knew it. And I was awake. She was going to catch me and put me in her pot.

Whoosh!

The sound and the blink of moonlight came again. A shiver snaked its way up my back. I needed to—

A hand clapped over my mouth. My eyes shot wide open in alarm. I tried to shout, to call out for Mom and Dad, but couldn't. I was trapped!

A scream built deep inside of me.

Jozlyn's face suddenly appeared very close to mine. She

looked as if she'd been sleeping. Her long hair was a mess and her blue eyes were squinting. She knelt on the floor between our beds.

She took her hand from my mouth. "Something's out there," she hissed. By *something*, she meant some*one*.

I nodded stiffly. "Witch Cleogha?"

Whoosh! The sound of bats zipped past again.

We both cringed at the noise. "Probably," Jozlyn whispered, glancing apprehensively at the window.

The light hadn't flickered this time but the noise had still come from somewhere close. Probably right over our house. Maybe over our room.

"We have to get Mom and Dad," she said.

Staring hard at the ceiling as if I'd be able to see right through it and spot the witch on her broom, I slid from my bed and joined Jozlyn on the floor. She grabbed my hand, but I didn't complain. Normally holding hands with your sister isn't very grown up, but this situation was different. I think it was all right to do when a witch was flying over our house.

"Let's go," Jozlyn urged. She clutched Rosie in her free hand. I had to admit that even with the doll, Jozlyn was being rather brave.

Side by side, we scuttled on our hands and knees toward the open door. Neither of us liked to sleep with it completely closed.

Our house was small like most houses in Tiller's Field, and our parents weren't rich. Dad worked in a bakery and mom helped another lady make cloaks, dresses, tunics, and bodices.

In the evenings, we would sit around the fireplace and listen to Dad tell stories about dragons, wizards, and knights who rescued princesses held captive by goblins and trolls.

Dad had a great imagination. He would sit in his big stuffed chair and entertain us for hours with his adventurous tales. I liked the scary ones best. Dad called them Knightscares, with a *k*. Kind of like nightmares only scarier.

Across from the fireplace was Mom and Dad's room. Their door was open, and that was odd. They usually slept with it closed.

The house was completely silent. Even the *whooshing* noise had stopped.

I turned to Jozlyn with an inquisitive look. She shrugged and nodded, sensing it too. Something wasn't right. The night had become too quiet.

As we inched forward, the floor creaked like a moaning spirit from one of Dad's stories. Then a more terrible sound drowned out everything else.

"*Ehh-he-he-he-he-heh!*" A witch's shrill cackle pierced the quiet night.

My heart jumped into my throat, pounding wildly, and my insides shivered so hard I thought they would become outsides.

Jozlyn whimpered softly and hugged Rosie to her chest. "In there," she said, pointing a shaky finger at our parents' bedroom.

She was right. The witch's cackle had come from straight ahead, from somewhere in our parents' room.

We climbed to our feet at the same time. We weren't thinking about being brave. We just acted. The witch had our parents, and it was up to us to do something about it.

We dashed into the dark bedroom and tripped on a blanket on the floor. It dragged us to the ground, and I landed hard on my elbow. Jozlyn tumbled down on top of me.

I looked at our parents' bed. I looked around the room. Both were empty.

Our parents were missing.

"*Ehh-he-he-he-he-heh!*" The witch cackled nearby.

Cleogha

3

Before we untangled ourselves from the blanket on the floor, Jozlyn and I heard the witch cackle again. The sound was close outside the window above our parents' bed. We flinched at the terrifying sound before creeping closer for a look.

My elbow bumped against the window ledge. "Be quiet, Josh," Jozlyn warned me. She was acting as if she was in charge the way big sisters do.

I scowled at her, rubbing my sore elbow, then carefully peeked out the window.

It looked like a town meeting or gathering of some kind was happening outside our house. Townsfolk stood in their night clothes talking in angry voices. There was a large crowd, and I recognized most of the people.

Mayor Garlo, with his bushy mustache and frumpy top

hat, was there. So were Mr. and Mrs. Cobblesole, the Chandler family with their baby Wick, Widow Marmelmaid, stocky Mr. Sootbeard the blacksmith, and many others.

Sheriff Logan stood nearby, too. As usual, he wore his leather battle armor and a long sword on his hip. He was the only person in town who carried a weapon at all times. I'd never seen him without one.

For some reason, he made me nervous. He had a dark look about him. I knew he was supposed to help people and protect the town. That's what the sheriff does. But he never laughed or smiled.

Right then, Sheriff Logan gripped a long dark broom painted with purple spots. He held it at arm's length the way a girl might hold a snake. The knuckles of his fingers were white.

I'd held Rosie that way before, so I knew how he felt.

With relief, I spotted my parents in the crowd. Dad had his arm around Mom's shoulders. That was a good sign. The two of them were always hugging or holding hands. Neither one of them looked afraid.

The townsfolk formed a ring around someone. I stared hard to make out the person and saw that it was Cleogha the witch.

Cleogha was ancient. Her snarled, long black hair was streaked with silver, and her round face was creased with wrinkles and covered in dark splotches like bruises on an apple. She had a hairy wart on the tip of her round nose.

She wore a shiny black dress trimmed with red at the collar and cuffs, long boots with toes that curled up, and a tall, pointed black hat with a wide brim.

The mayor pointed at her angrily. His face was almost as red as the trim on her dress.

"Now listen here, Witch Cleogha," he told her angrily. "You're disturbing the peace with all that flying to and fro. My, my. There's laws against that sort of behavior." He puffed up his chest and his mustache flapped with every word he spoke.

"But ... but Mayor Garlo, 'tis a witch's *eh-he-he-he-*holiday," Cleogha argued in her cackling voice. "'Tis Cauldron Cooker's Night. I should be allowed to celebrate. 'Tis a free town, after all."

The crowd of people muttered their objections. No one seemed convinced by Cleogha's argument.

"You woke our son," Mr. Chandler accused in a grumpy tone. Baby Wick fidgeted in his mother's arms.

"Aye, disturbed my work, too, you did," the blacksmith, Mr. Sootbeard, growled in a deep voice. "I was just finishing up a new shield for the sheriff here when you flew by and surprised me. The shield's ruined. I'll have to start again."

I was getting a bad feeling. I looked over at Jozlyn and

19

saw that she was frowning. I think she felt the same as I did.

The mayor waved his arms, calling for silence before he spoke again. "My, my. Tiller's Field is indeed a free town, Witch Cleogha, but your rights may not infringe upon anyone else's freedom. I'm afraid that I cannot allow you to ride your broom after sunset."

Something mysterious flashed in Cleogha's eyes. Something devious. Even in the moonlight I could see that she was up to no good. Her eyes seemed to glow and she took a deep breath.

She was going to cast a spell, I realized. I grabbed Jozlyn by the shoulder and pulled her back with me away from the window.

Broomsnake Stick

4

Cleogha's hands shot up and she waved them furiously. In a loud voice, she chanted the words to a spell:

> Slither scale, hiss and spit.
> Wiggle tail, slap and hit.
>
> To my hand, I now command,
> Magic make that broom a snake!

At the end of her chant, she tossed some glittering dust high into the air. It sparkled and hissed like a serpent as it fell. Some of it landed on the sheriff and he shouted in alarm.

I gulped. Whatever was happening, it was bad. Sheriff Logan was as brave as a dragon. He wouldn't cry out for just anything.

The crowd gasped and Jozlyn shrieked loudly in my ear. Everyone took a step back, their eyes on the sheriff and on what lashed about in his outstretched hand.

The purple-spotted broom was gone. The sheriff now held a big snake with a long forked tongue.

Deep green and covered with purple splotches just like the broom had been, the snake thrashed violently in the sheriff's hand. Its tongue shot in and out of its mouth menacingly.

Sheriff Logan hurled the snake to the ground with a gasp, jumped back, and whipped out his long sword in one blazing motion. There was hardly time to see him do it.

Shing! His blade whisked free of its scabbard.

"Look out!" Jozlyn screamed. She held Rosie in front of her for protection like one of Cleogha's charms against trolls.

I hoped Rosie protected against snakes.

The snake wiggled and slithered toward Cleogha. Sheriff Logan leaped forward like a pouncing cat to chop the scaly thing in half, but Cleogha bent down and snatched the snake up in her wrinkled hands.

The snake flicked its tongue across her skin the way a puppy licks his owner.

Disgusting! I thought.

Cleogha held the snake above her head and the crowd

watched in fear. "End the doom! Snake to broom!" she shouted, and the snake went very still, becoming as straight as a knight's lance. It glowed brightly and I had to shield my eyes.

When the light faded and I could look again, Cleogha held nothing but her broom.

"This broom be mine. You were wrong to take it from me," Cleogha declared to the stunned onlookers.

I was amazed. I'd never seen actual magic performed before, except for Wizard Ast's tricks on Trooping Fairy Day. This was different. It was real and terrifying.

Mayor Garlo adjusted the top hat on his head and stepped forward. He tugged on his long white mustache with one hand.

"My, my. Riding your broom after sunset *and* casting spells in the moonlight. Even on Cauldron Cooker's Night, these things cannot be tolerated. You leave me no choice, Witch Cleogha. I hereby revoke your license to do business in Tiller's Field."

The crowd murmured again, this time in approval. I couldn't help agreeing with them. Cleogha was dangerous.

Sheriff Logan still held his sword before him. He wasn't taking any chances.

"And furthermore," the red-faced mayor continued, "you must leave Tiller's Field at once and never return. We cannot tolerate your snakes and spells within the city limits.

You are ordered to go. Now!"

Cleogha cackled her piercing witch's cackle and another shiver slithered up my spine. I couldn't stop thinking about the green and purple snake, and about the witch's magic.

What else could she do? Could she turn me into a snake? Could she turn me into something even worse?

"So be it, Mayor," Cleogha hissed, "but I will be back. Tiller's Field be my home and I will return."

She straddled the broom-that-was-also-a-snake and floated up into the air.

"I will return!" she spat, pointing at the mayor. Then she rotated slowly and pointed at various people in the crowd. "Mark my words, all of you!" she shouted, kicking her legs like a little kid on a rocking horse.

Suddenly she spun to face Jozlyn and me. We crouched low, but it was too late. Cleogha had spotted us. I heard Mom gasp.

Dad shouted at us. "Jozlyn, Josh—*run!*"

Jozlyn raced back into the living room but my legs wouldn't respond. I was frozen in place, paralyzed by the witch's stare. Her dark eyes made my skin crawl, and I stopped breathing.

"I will be back, young man," Cleogha promised, pointing at me this time. "Mark my words. I'll be back. Even if you are dead before I do!"

Dead? I repeated to myself. *Dead?* What had I done to

deserve death?

Cleogha cackled again and swooped over the crowd toward our house. "I'll be back. You mark my words."

There was nothing I could do. Witch Cleogha had decided that I was her enemy. She was going to get revenge. She was going to get me.

I collapsed weakly and fell onto the bed.

Cleogha wanted me dead!

Cat Got Your Nose?

5

In the morning, my excitement over Trooping Fairy Day put the fears and thoughts of Cleogha out of my head. I had better things to think about. Fun things.

Little did I know that I would soon be thinking about the witch a lot.

I jumped out of bed and let out a loud whoop. I was so excited. The day had finally arrived. No witches, no school, no chores—just fun all day and night.

Jozlyn stirred in her bed and squinted sleepily at me. "Hush! You have the manners of a garbage-gobbling goblin," she scolded as I cavorted wildly about my bed.

Older sisters never seem to get as excited about things as their younger brothers.

I took a deep breath and jumped from my bed to hers. I continued to bounce up and down like … well, like a garbage-gobbling goblin.

I sang a silly song to go along with my crazy dance.

> Summer's here, but I don't care.
> I smell garbage in the air.
> Chew and burp,
> Gobble, slurp—
> I'm a goblin, so beware!

Thunk! Jozlyn's pillow whacked me in the face. I collapsed on her bed and she tickled me. We both laughed.

Mom and Dad peeked into our room just then. They were smiling and dressed in fancy outfits that Mom had sewn for special occasions. They looked very dapper.

"Are you two goblins ready for breakfast?" Dad asked with a grin.

"I'm not a goblin," Jozlyn protested, pretending to pout. She knew Dad was teasing, so she teased right back. "But *he* is, so I'll eat his share of breakfast!"

She gave me a shove and then jumped out of bed and ran giggling through the door and into the kitchen.

We all ate in a hurry, cleaned up, and left. No matter how eager we were to get going, Mom insisted that we clean up. *Work first and play later*, she always said. I guess it made sense to get the hard stuff out of the way.

The walk to the festival grounds took forever. The grounds weren't that far away but every step seemed to get us only an inch closer.

I think Mom walked slow on purpose. She kept stopping to point out flowers and butterflies. Jozlyn acted as if she was interested but I knew she was just trying to act more grown-up.

I ran ahead to scout our path, then I dashed back to report my findings. "Almost to Mosswood Bridge," I announced.

Mosswood Bridge crossed Gurgleburp Creek at the edge of town. The creek was named Gurgleburp because of the noise it made passing through a patch of rapids under the bridge. *Gurgle*, the water went down into the rocks. Then *burp,* it hiccupped out the other side.

My friend Connor was waiting for me outside the festival grounds. He was the one who claimed to have seen a troll. He leaned against the wooden gate while people made their way inside.

Connor was my age but had short blond hair. He was also a lot bigger than I was. His dad was a knight, so I guess muscles ran in the family.

"Morning, Connor," I said cheerfully when I saw him.

"That's *Sir* Connor to you, peasant," Connor replied. He was always calling people *peasant*. Anyone who wasn't a knight was a peasant in his eyes. That made Connor a peasant because he wasn't a knight, but I didn't point that out to him.

I turned to Mom, who was pointing at a bird's nest.

29

"Mom, can I go with Connor? I promise to be back in time for the parade."

"Sure, dear," Mom smiled. "But no exploring the woods."

The festival and parade took place at the edge of Everleaf Woods. The edge of the woods was safe, but the inside was dark and spooky and led to Croneswart Swamp. The swamp was just about the darkest and spookiest place there was.

"Great!" I shouted, turning to Connor, but Dad called me.

"You'll need this," he said, tossing something shiny into the air. It sparkled in a high arc, and I caught it when it came down. It was a silver penny.

Silver! This was going to be the best Trooping Fairy Day ever.

"Thanks, Dad!" I beamed.

"Enjoy yourself, you rich goblin, and be sure to meet us by the fountain in time for the parade," Dad instructed as Connor and I dashed through the gate.

People wandered everywhere, shopping, talking, and smiling. Jugglers tossed colorful balls and knives in the air. Bards sang songs, strumming and tooting on instruments. Acrobats in silly costumes and caps with long floppy tops bounded down the streets doing cartwheels and back-flips. Food vendors waved scrumptious-looking treats and candies for all to see.

There was even a little black cat with one silver ear wearing a red collar scurrying in and out around people's feet.

I bought some gooey taffy and foamy green punch that bubbled like a science experiment for Connor and me. We walked around for a long time watching people, laughing at the street performers, playing games, and talking with friends wherever we saw them.

We bought more snacks, too, and pretty soon our stomachs hurt so much that we really did feel like gobbling goblins.

"Josh, look at that crazy cat," Connor said. He pointed at the little black cat sitting a few feet away from us.

People had to step around it because it refused to budge. It sat in the middle of the roadway, just staring.

I shrugged. "Probably hungry," I told Connor. I squatted down in front of the cat. "Sorry, kitty, we don't have any treats for you." It was true. I'd spent all of my silver, and we'd eaten all of the treats.

The cat stared at me, blinking slowly. Then it jumped up and swatted my nose.

Cat Thief

6

I fell back on my rump. People laughed and pointed. The little cat had knocked me down. How embarrassing!

I rubbed my nose where the cat had scratched me. It hurt more than a little scratch should hurt and sort of tingled.

The cat scampered back, then stopped and turned around. "Meow," it said.

I waved a hand at it angrily. "Go away!"

Connor stomped his feet. "Be gone, peasant," he ordered the cat.

"Meow," it said again. It didn't seem afraid of us.

I stood up and kicked at the dirt. I didn't like the idea of people laughing at me, and I wanted to go somewhere else.

The cat was giving me a weird feeling. It kept staring at me as if it could read my mind. I hoped it could read the mean thoughts I was thinking about it.

"Come on, Connor, let's go," I said grumpily.

We met my parents and Jozlyn by the fountain a little while later. Connor called me a peasant one more time, said goodbye, and went off to find his own family.

Mom and Dad sat with their backs against the fountain. Lots of other people did, too. The fountain was short and round and had a stone unicorn in the center. Water sprayed from the unicorn's horn. I think Mom and Dad picked the spot because of the unicorn. They knew Jozlyn loved horses and a unicorn was the next best thing.

Jozlyn and I sat in front of our parents. A row of children stretched to both sides of us. Kids always got the front-row seats.

Lights of blue, red, pink, and green suddenly flashed in the trees to our left. They sparkled like shining raindrops, floating gracefully down from the highest branches to the ground.

For some reason, they made me think of Cleogha's magic dust. I didn't want to think about the witch but I couldn't help myself.

"Ooooh, they're so pretty," Jozlyn gasped. Her eyes were wide and Rosie sat propped in her lap. Jozlyn claimed Rosie needed a good seat, too, because she was a pixie and wanted to watch her friends in the parade.

Obviously Jozlyn wasn't thinking of magic dust or anything else from last night.

The fairies continued to flutter down. I'd seen the parade enough times to know that the lights were really fairies holding tiny candles. Fairies have wings, so gliding down from a tree isn't a problem for them.

Another disturbing thought popped into my head, this one about flying. Cleogha the witch could fly, too, just like the fairies.

Why am I thinking about Cleogha so much? I wondered. *First her dust and now her flying broom. I should be enjoying the parade.*

I fidgeted and took a deep breath. The fairies had landed and were skipping back and forth through the grass. They zigzagged like a snake—

A snake! I saw Cleogha's green and purple snake in my mind. I just couldn't stop thinking about what had happened on Cauldron Cooker's Night.

"Meow," the little black cat said suddenly from out of nowhere. It was rubbing against Jozlyn's knee, and my sister scratched it behind its silver ear.

I stared at the cat and it stared at me. "What do you want?" I asked, making a face. The scratch on my nose started to tingle again.

"Help me-ow," the cat replied. Then it jumped into Jozlyn's lap, snatched Rosie in its mouth, and raced into the woods.

Help Me-ow

7

Stunned, I watched frozen and silent as the cat bounded speedily through the crowd. In no time it disappeared into Everleaf Woods.

I couldn't believe what had happened. Had the cat really said *Help me-ow*? Had it really taken Jozlyn's doll and run off?

Everything had happened so fast. The cat had spoken, I'd blinked, and then it had taken Rosie and dashed off. It had all taken place in no more than a second or two.

It was unreal.

But not to Jozlyn. She was shrieking at the top of her lungs and bumping her way through the crowd after the cat. Tears streaked her face and she held the pleats of her yellow dress bunched in her hands so she wouldn't trip.

"Stop that cat!" she howled over and over in a high-pitched wail.

Dad jumped up and went after her immediately, muttering apologies whenever he accidentally bumped into someone.

"Pardon me, milady" and "Excuse me, milord," he said, over and over. Dad was always polite even when he was in a hurry.

An elderly lady was trying to move out of Dad's way, but kept moving in the same direction he tried to go. First left, *bonk*. They bumped into each other. Then right, *bonk*. They bumped again.

Finally, Dad wrapped his arms around the woman's waist, heaved her up like a sack of grain, and turned in a half circle.

He set her back on her feet with a "Deepest apologies, madam, forgive me" and a quick bow. Then he zipped off after Jozlyn.

When Dad vanished around a corner, Mom tapped me on the shoulder and told me to get up. It was time to go. She knew Jozlyn. If we didn't find Rosie, there'd be no making my sister happy.

The parade was ruined because of Jozlyn's doll and that weird cat, and I couldn't help thinking mean thoughts. Of course I didn't know it then, but that doll was going to save us all.

We looked for Rosie a long time. We searched under

wagons, in corners packed with crates, and through the cramped rows of merchant's stalls. We even went to the edge of Everleaf Woods and called "Here, kitty-kitty" for what seemed like hours.

In the end, we came home empty-handed. We hadn't seen any sign of the cat. Rosie was gone.

Jozlyn was quiet and had a strange look on her face the whole way home. It reminded me of the look Cleogha had when she'd pointed at me and said she would return.

It was eerie to have my sister remind me of a witch.

Jozlyn went to sleep without saying a word, and I followed her to bed soon after. Trooping Fairy Day was over for another year. Instead of being so worn out that I fell asleep right away, I kept hearing the cat whisper "Help me-ow" as I tossed and turned.

Help me-ow.

Help. Me.

It took a long time for me to fall asleep, but it seemed only a minute after that when Jozlyn clamped her hand over my mouth. It was her favorite trick lately.

"I'm going after Rosie," she told me seriously, and I came instantly awake.

8

Jozlyn was wearing a pair of my hose along with a plain brown tunic and boots. She had a small bundle draped over her shoulder.

She looked serious. She sounded serious. But I still had to ask.

"Are you serious?"

She shot me a look but didn't say anything.

"How did Mom and Dad agree to this?" I pressed. "We aren't supposed to go into Everleaf Woods. Not ever."

That was true. Kids weren't allowed to go anywhere near Everleaf Woods except during the festival. The woods were too close to Croneswart Swamp, and dark things lived in the swamp.

"They don't know. Duh!" With a determined look on her face, Jozlyn adjusted the bundle on her shoulder. "Now are you coming with me or not?"

"Yeah, yeah," I said, climbing out of bed to get dressed. Her look told me for certain. She was going. Someone had to keep an eye on her. "But what's in the bundle?"

She shrugged. "Just cheese and yesterday's bread. I thought we might get hungry. Who knows how long it'll take to find Rosie."

I groaned. Jozlyn had planned for a long trip.

"Be as quiet as possible," she told me in her syrupy big-sister voice. "We can't wake Mom and Dad."

I crossed my eyes and gave her a stupid look. "Really? Is that why it's called sneaking?"

Jozlyn pinched me, and I had to bite my tongue to keep from crying out. "Careful or your face will freeze like that," she scolded, sounding like Mom.

Sisters, I thought and rolled my eyes.

I silently finished getting dressed and then we headed outside. I was starting to feel a little excited. Well, excited and nervous.

Today we were going to have an adventure like in one of Dad's stories. I pretended that the cat was a loathsome monster that had kidnapped Princess Rosie. Jozlyn and I were heroes sent to rescue the poor princess even if we had to risk the dangers of Croneswart Swamp.

But the fun of the adventure wore off quickly. Rain had fallen during the night, and thick fog hung in the air. We could hardly see more than an arm's length away.

To top it off, the sun wasn't even all the way up. Its dim light was grey and weak as if it wasn't sure whether to brighten up after the rain or to keep hiding behind the clouds.

The streets were suspiciously quiet, too. Our footsteps echoed loudly in every direction as we walked through town. They were the only sound.

It felt as if we were walking through a cemetery at night. There was no sound or movement except for Jozlyn and me clomping around where we weren't supposed to be.

The quiet made the town feel abandoned and dead. Normally we wouldn't be able to hear our own footsteps. They would be lost in the busy sounds of life in the town.

But today there was only the sound of our boots slapping on the ground. They clomped hollowly like knocks on an empty coffin. Only a coffin wasn't supposed to be empty and neither was our town.

Clomp-clomp, went my boots on the cobblestone streets. *Click-click*, went Jozlyn's. Then they echoed dreamily. *Clomp-click ... clomp- click ... clomp-click ...*

I picked up the pace and Jozlyn followed, clinging to my sleeve. The echoes grew louder as we sped up, but at least it felt like we were getting somewhere.

At last we came to the sheriff's office, the last building at the edge of town. The building was dark like all the rest we had passed and that didn't seem like a good sign. Of all the people in town, the sheriff shouldn't be sleeping late. Who would protect us if Cleogha decided to come back like she'd promised?

Jozlyn gasped and pulled hard on my sleeve. "*W*-what's that?" she stammered, pointing straight ahead.

Something moved in the fog on Mosswood Bridge.

I squinted, trying to get a good look. The something was a tall, dark shape moving quickly toward us.

Suddenly I remembered Connor's story about the troll. He'd said that he'd seen it fishing from the bridge.

I grabbed Jozlyn's arm. We had to run.

"Troll!" I managed to gasp, and Jozlyn's eyes popped open wide. Her face went white.

The dark shape on the bridge was a troll just like in Connor's story.

Pointy End First

9

Jozlyn whimpered, or it might have been me. I didn't know or really care. I was more worried about the troll coming our way. I wouldn't blame anyone for whimpering at a time like that.

Trolls were mean, ugly, and always hungry. They had moldy green skin covered in warts. Each of their two heads had a big mouth full of big teeth. Long claws tipped their hands and feet.

Worst of all, they'd eat anything, especially children. We're crunchy snacks to them.

"This way!" I said in my best hero's voice. I still had a hold of Jozlyn's arm and gave it a mighty tug, but I pulled so hard that I knocked both of us down. Some hero I was.

Jozlyn heaved me off of her and scrambled to her feet. She ran toward the sheriff's office.

I followed clumsily. For some reason, my legs and feet felt really heavy, and I couldn't seem to catch my breath.

The troll was getting closer. I could hear its feet slapping wetly on the damp planks of the bridge. It would be in the street very soon.

Slap, slap.

We skidded to a stop behind the far wall of the building, around the corner from the street. Both of us were panting, and Jozlyn's long hair was a mess. A barrel stood at the edge of the building to catch rain that dripped from the roof when it stormed.

We crouched behind the barrel and held our breath, waiting and watching for the troll to shamble by. At least we hoped it would shamble by without seeing us.

"I wish I had a sword so I could vanquish the troll," I told Jozlyn quietly. I was thinking of the heroes in Dad's stories. They were always vanquishing trolls and ogres and other beasts with a sword.

And I liked that word. *Vanquish.* It meant to defeat.

"Like you'd know what to do with a sword," Jozlyn huffed between big breaths.

"Sure I would," I said defensively. "Pointy end goes in the troll." Everybody knew that. Jozlyn just had to act as if she was smarter than I was.

"Oh, and you think it's easy to stab something that doesn't want to be stabbed?" Jozlyn rolled her eyes at me.

43

"Stop being such a *boy* and keep quiet."

I thought about that. Maybe she had a point. I know I wouldn't stand around waiting to be stabbed. A troll probably wouldn't either.

But I still thought vanquishing sounded like a good idea and that I could do it to some dumb troll.

The troll's footsteps grew louder. Jozlyn and I crouched lower and flattened ourselves against the building. We couldn't see the troll but it was out there.

Slap, slap.

It was very close now and moving fast. Its heavy feet thudded on the cobblestone in unison to the thumping of my heart.

Fog swirled on the street. The troll was about to appear, and Jozlyn and I sucked in our breath to scream.

10

The fog swirled like smoke and a man stepped through it. A man, not a troll! I almost sighed with relief until I saw who it was and how he looked.

It was an angry Sheriff Logan. His face was scrunched up in a scowl and he held his sword in one hand. The blade glistened with something wet that looked, something shiny along its sharp edges.

Blood, I realized. His sword was covered with blood. I just *knew* the sheriff wasn't to be trusted.

I wanted to turn invisible. Why did the mysterious figure have to be the unsmiling sheriff with a bloody sword? I think I'd almost rather have seen a troll. At least a troll was just a big, stupid brute.

But not Sheriff Logan. The sheriff was an expert warrior. That was what the town paid him to be. Only now, he had murder in his eyes and blood on his sword.

Something darted in the fog on the other side of the street. It was small, dark, and very fast.

The sheriff stopped immediately and dropped into a crouch. His hawk eyes narrowed as he turned to face the threat. He didn't wait long.

The dark shape sprinted from the fog toward him and I gasped. So did Jozlyn. It was the cat with the one silver ear. It meowed loudly as it scampered toward the sheriff.

"Where is your mistress, fiend?" he demanded, swinging his sword threateningly.

The cat meowed again but didn't stop. I don't think it was interested in what the sheriff had to say. It dashed right between his legs and headed for us.

Jozlyn pulled me closer to her and I felt her shiver. She didn't trust the sheriff any more than I did, and she hated that cat. It had stolen Rosie, so it was her enemy.

At the last moment, the cat turned sharply and raced past us in the fog. It snarled as it went by, and its ears were pressed flat against its head.

Sheriff Logan sprinted right behind. He charged after the cat, pumping his arms and legs. "Come back, fiend!" he yelled. His long cloak flapped behind him like a flag.

If he weren't so dangerous, I'd say he looked like a hero from one of Dad's stories.

Jozlyn and I waited until the sheriff's voice and the sound

of his boots faded into silence. Then we finally breathed
again. I hadn't realized I could hold my breath so long.

"Let's get out of here," Jozlyn urged. "With the cat gone,
we should be able to find Rosie easy enough. She's probably scared and lying in the dirt somewhere all alone."

Suddenly I felt angry. How could Jozlyn think of her doll
at a time like this? Rosie was a dumb doll, not a person or
a real pixie. There were more important things to worry
about.

I climbed to my feet and grabbed Jozlyn's shoulders with
both of my hands. "What do you mean? We've got to
wake Mom and Dad. Didn't you see the sheriff's sword? It
was covered with blood!"

Instead of agreeing, Jozlyn stared at me with a blank look
on her face. I knew immediately that she hadn't seen the
blood. If she had, she would be running already.

Instead she laughed and pointed to the east, toward the
rising sun. "You're such a … silly kid," she said, chuckling.

Confused, I looked over my shoulder and down the street
toward home. The fog was thinning and I could see the
reddish-orange glow of the sun painted brightly across the
sky. It reflected off buildings and the signs hanging about
town.

The reflections looked kind of like blood. Kind of the
way the sheriff's sword had looked.

I sighed to myself, feeling stupid. How many times was I

going to make dumb mistakes? Hearing the cat say, "Help me-ow." Believing Connor's goofy story about the troll. Seeing blood on Sheriff Logan's sword. I was scaring myself with my overactive imagination.

What was wrong with me? I was confusing Dad's stories with real life, but I should have known better. Trolls didn't fish from bridges. Cats didn't talk. I was getting things mixed up and needed to settle down.

Feeling sorry for myself, I hung my head. I should have stayed in bed.

Jozlyn punched my shoulder playfully. "Come on, little brother. Let's find Rosie. I bet Sheriff Logan takes care of that cat." She was trying to make me feel better, but I wasn't going to feel better that fast.

I nodded silently. I didn't feel much like talking.

We brushed ourselves off and headed down the street toward Mosswood Bridge. From there it wasn't far to the festival grounds and Everleaf Woods.

As we walked, the sun continued to rise. It warmed our backs and cast long shadows in front of us. The fog thinned as we went, too. The day was turning out to be nice after all.

Now, I thought to myself, *if I can quit seeing and hearing monsters all over the place, everything will be all right*. I needed to remember that I wasn't a hero and that life wasn't always an adventure.

Jozlyn hummed a little tune while we walked and pointed out a butterfly the way Mom had done the day before. Only today, I stopped to watch it for a bit.

Its colorful wings were tiny and delicate, like paper pressed so thin that you could almost see through it. I could hardly believe that something that was once a fuzzy caterpillar could sprout wings and learn to fly.

It was really pretty amazing if you thought about it. Maybe it was a kind of magic.

I smiled and caught up with Jozlyn. I was starting to feel better. The sun was shining and the fog had disappeared. I even spotted an odd blue and orange spider, and pointed it out to Jozlyn.

Of course, that was right when everything went wrong. That was right before Cleogha returned.

Hop Along, Flop Along

11

A shadow passed in front of the sun just as we reached the festival gate. We turned around in alarm. The unpleasant memories of the frightening shape on the bridge and the strange scene between the sheriff and the silver-eared cat were too fresh in our minds for us not to be a little jittery.

Jozlyn was first to notice that the shadow had been a passing cloud. "*Bwawk-bwawk*," she said like a chicken, flapping her elbows with her hands on her hips. "Did the puffy white cloud scare you?"

I was about to say, *Not as much as you wearing my clothes,* but the words stuck in my throat. There was something else in the sky besides clouds.

A tiny dark splotch zipped back and forth like a fly. It looked to be right over the center of town.

I watched but didn't panic. I was too worried about

making a fool of myself again. The thing in the sky definitely wasn't a troll or a talking cat, and I thought it best to wait to say anything until I knew for sure what it was.

Jozlyn noticed me staring and turned to look again herself. She immediately pointed at the splotch and asked, "What is it?"

"Shhh!" I hissed quietly. I was concentrating on the splotch. I still didn't know what it was, but I knew one thing.

It was getting bigger.

I had a bad feeling. The splotch couldn't be a bird because birds didn't zip back and forth that way. It had to be a witch on her broom.

"Let's find a place to hide—fast," I urged. I was genuinely afraid now. Bigger meant that the splotch was getting closer. "It's coming this way."

"There!" Jozlyn exclaimed, pointing at a big willow tree with long drooping branches. The branches dangled all the way to the ground and were thick with leaves.

"Perfect," I said. "Let's go." Jozlyn was already running, but I paused to take one more look at the splotch. It was much bigger now.

"Josh, hurry up! It's going to see you."

My sister was behind the willow's branches. Only her head peeked through the leaves. I ran. I had a pretty good idea of what the splotch was, and hiding was exactly the thing to do.

I didn't bother to slow down when I reached the tree. I barged right through its branches with my arms out straight like I was diving into water. Leaves slapped my face and vines snagged my clothes. I tripped and crashed into the trunk with a thud.

Panting and feeling a little dizzy, I rolled over to face Jozlyn. Little scrapes and cuts covered my face and hands. Even the scratch on my nose from the cat was tingling again.

"I think it's the witch," I panted fearfully. "I think it's Cleogha on her broom."

Jozlyn squinted at me then stuck her head back through the wall of leaves. She made a little squeak and then popped her head back inside right away. Her face was pale.

"You're right. It sure looks like her." Her bottom lip quivered as if she was about to cry. "What are we going to do, Josh? Cleogha hates us."

Right then, I don't think I would have felt better next to anyone else. As my sister, Jozlyn had decided that if the witch hated me, then she hated Jozlyn, too. Jozlyn and I were a team.

I wanted to thank her but couldn't think of anything good to say. All that came out of my mouth was, "We'll be safe here. She can't see us."

I hoped I was right.

Jozlyn was about to say something more when the witch let out her terrible cackle from right overhead.

"*Eh-he-he-he-heh!*" Some of the leaves around us rustled as if blown by the wind.

"Hide while you can, little ones," came the witch's raspy voice. "It won't be long now."

We had to do something. The tree felt like a cage. The witch had us trapped.

On our hands and knees, we scuttled to the far side of the willow and paused at the edge to take a deep breath.

"Jozlyn, we're not far from the woods. If we can make it into the trees, the witch won't be able to spot us."

It was our only hope. I hated the idea of going into Everleaf Woods, but I hated it less than the idea of the witch catching us.

The witch cackled again. "Come out, come out! You won't like what I'll do if you make me come in there."

Jozlyn swallowed and her face took on that serious look that it had when she'd told me was going after Rosie. She looked afraid and serious at the same time.

"Let's go," she said steadily. Her voice didn't shake at all like mine had. I think she might really be braver than I am. "Race you there."

She was on her feet and through the hanging branches before I could blink. I'd wanted to say, *On the count of three*, but there wasn't time.

I zoomed after her and shot through the wall of branches. The edge of the woods wasn't far. I could make it. Jozlyn was almost there.

"*Eh-he-he-he-heh!*" the witch cackled. Her voice sounded close enough to be a shout right in my ear.

The ground raced passed beneath my charging feet. Tears from the wind blurred my vision. I was running as fast as I could.

"Target practice!" the witch exclaimed, and I could hear her chanting the words to a spell.

Jozlyn reached the woods and disappeared in the cluster of trees. At least she was safe.

Almost there, I told myself, risking a glance over my shoulder.

The witch hovered about twenty feet in the air on her broom. I could see her legs and curl-toed boots but not much else. She was wearing a long black cloak that whipped about her like the flames of a roaring fire.

Her chanted words made my ears itch.

> Hop along, flop along,
> Croak and eat flies.
> Jump away, thump away,
> Be you frog size!

An explosive crackling burst all around the witch, and then a beam of sparking green light shot down toward me.

I shouted in terror and dove headfirst into the woods. The beam of light crashed into a tree trunk just over my back. If I hadn't jumped, it would have hit me dead on.

The tree exploded in a cloud of green smoke. Bark and leaves erupted into the air. Sap and twigs pelted me like stinging insects.

When the smoke cleared, the tree was gone and a big green frog sat in its place, croaking loudly.

I climbed to my feet and ran deeper into the woods like I've never run before. The witch had turned the tree into a frog, but she'd meant to do it to me.

Her triumphant cackle followed me into the leafy darkness.

12

I charged recklessly through the woods. I twisted around trees, leaped over roots and fallen logs, and ducked under low branches. I didn't pay attention to which way I went or to what I passed. I had to get away from the witch. Nothing else mattered.

When I tripped for about the tenth time, I stayed down and gasped for breath with my head between my knees. I couldn't run anymore.

I thought about Jozlyn and hoped she'd managed to escape. I didn't want a frog for a sister. But I needed to get out of the woods before worrying about that. If I didn't find my way back, I wouldn't see Jozlyn again at all, frog or not.

Just then I needed to worry about where I was. I had never been in Everleaf Woods before.

Towering trees stretched endlessly in every direction, and

strange noises echoed all around. Trees creaked, insects chirped, leaves rustled, and things I couldn't see scurried in the undergrowth.

I didn't know which way to go, but I couldn't stay where I was. I felt itchy and hot, and I imagined hundreds of hungry eyes staring at me and wondering how I would taste.

Climbing tiredly back to my feet, I called for Jozlyn. I cupped my hands around my mouth and called again. I turned in circles calling over and over.

I heard nothing from her. No response.

I'm lost in the woods, I thought and took a few aimless steps. *Now how do I get out?*

I looked at the enormous trees soaring high above and felt small and alone. The trees' wide trunks were craggy and covered with moss. They were hundreds of years old.

Moss! That was it. Dad had once told me that moss only grew on the north sides of trees.

Trying not to think about what might be squirming in the moss, I leaned against the shaggy trunk of a tree.

"Please be right," I whispered. I'm not sure if I meant me or Dad's advice.

With my back against the tree, looking straight ahead was north. That meant home was to my right, to the east. I knew that much from having seen the rising sun earlier that morning.

I trotted east, slow enough so that I wouldn't trip but fast enough to drown out the unpleasant noises in the woods.

Every few dozen steps I stopped to check my progress. First I held my breath and listened for the witch, then I searched for more mossy trunks. When I didn't hear the witch, I started moving again.

I hoped I was making good time because I was starting to get hungry. I thought about the bread and cheese in Jozlyn's bundle. I hoped she still had them.

Most of all, I hoped that Jozlyn wasn't a frog. How would I explain that to Mom and Dad? We were forbidden to enter the woods. I couldn't imagine how many rules we would have broken by getting Jozlyn turned into a frog.

That's when I saw Rosie. What was left of her anyway. She was lying in a tangled heap in the dirt just as Jozlyn had suspected.

Kneeling, I gently scooped up the battered pixie doll. Her pink dress was in tatters, and dirt and little twigs were sticking out of her yellow hair. One of her wings was torn and clung limply to her back. Tiny bite marks covered her body.

Jozlyn would be heartbroken. I couldn't let her see Rosie in such bad shape.

Pulling up the bottom of my tunic, I carefully wrapped the doll in the loose material and stuffed the extra into my hose. Mom could fix Rosie later. Then I would show Jozlyn that I'd found her.

"Josh, is that you?" It was Jozlyn's voice from not too far off. She sounded scared. "Please Josh, if that's you, answer me. Cleogha is gone. I think she gave up and left."

Relief washed over me. We were safe again and I'd found Rosie. We'd survived a real adventure.

I didn't know it then, but our adventure was just beginning.

"Yes, Jozlyn!" I called back. "It's me. I'm coming." I double-checked Rosie's spot inside my tunic. She seemed safe and out of sight. "Please keep talking so I can find you."

To Jozlyn's repeated calls of "Over here!" and "This way, Josh!" I managed to find her without more trouble. Luckily, she was still near the edge of the woods. I could see sunshine and sky from where she waited for me.

I'm not ashamed to say that I hugged Jozlyn when I saw her. I was glad we were both safe and not frogs.

"We have to get home, Josh," Jozlyn told me after we'd looked each other over. "The witch said something about Tiller's Field. I'm worried that she's planning something awful."

Nearby, the frog that Cleogha had transformed from a tree croaked again. Jozlyn and I sharply turned our heads to face one another. We both had the same idea.

If Cleogha could turn a tree into a frog, what could she do to the townsfolk of Tiller's Field?

Vanishing Act

13

"Wait," I cautioned. "Let's not panic. We don't know for sure that Cleogha is planning something. We can't let our imaginations get the best of us."

For once, I was trying to think things through. The last thing we needed to do was worry over nothing. The witch chasing us into the woods was real and had just happened. That was terrible enough to think about.

"You're right," Jozlyn agreed. Her face brightened with a small smile. "Maybe Cleogha spotted us and just couldn't resist a little mischief." She wagged her fingers at me mysteriously.

I nodded and grinned a little myself. "So we should hurry back and warn Mom and Dad. They'll want to know what happened, even if we left home without permission."

I wasn't thinking about getting in trouble for breaking

rules. Having a witch chase you is more important.

"We should tell Mayor Garlo, too," Jozlyn added. "He'll want to hear about our adventure. He might even send Sheriff Logan out to arrest Cleogha."

"Good thinking," I told her. I was feeling much better. So much better that I remembered about being hungry. "Now what about that bread and cheese?"

We nibbled breakfast as we walked home. Well, Jozlyn nibbled. I gobbled like a goblin.

Sunshine warmed our faces, and a few fluffy white clouds floated in the sky. There was no sign of more rain or fog. I felt pretty good about that.

It would have been a typical, perfect summer morning if not for the nagging feeling in my gut. Even though Jozlyn and I had decided not to worry about Cleogha, I still did.

I couldn't help it. Butterflies fluttered in my stomach faster and faster with every step we took toward home.

Whenever I glanced at Jozlyn, she seemed to be concentrating on something unpleasant, too. Her lips were pressed tightly together, and her blue eyes were paying no attention to the wide path beneath our feet.

"There's something on the bridge," Jozlyn said suddenly, pointing ahead. My stomach did a double flip. The butterflies were bats now.

This time, the something on the bridge wasn't a troll or a man. It was shiny, lumpy pile.

61

We hurried onto the bridge. The creek below gurgled and burped just like its name, and the damp wood creaked under our feet.

The pile was a cluster of loose weapons. There was a curved dagger, a deer-hide quiver full of arrows, and a long sword with a polished golden handle. All of the weapons were sharp and handsome, expensive. But they were just lying on the bridge in a heap.

I recognized the sword immediately. It belonged to Sheriff Logan.

"Jozlyn, that's—" I began.

"I know. It's the sheriff's." She prodded the pile of weapons with her toe. "All of these are his. But why are they sitting here on the bridge?"

Still trying not to jump to conclusions, I said, "Let's keep looking,"

Walking close together, we crossed Mosswood Bridge and entered town. The streets were suspiciously empty of people the same way they had been earlier in the morning.

The only difference was that there were curious piles everywhere. Lots of them. Sacks of spilled vegetables, overturned buckets, broken crates, bits and pieces of cracked pottery, and woven baskets full of laundry lay discarded on the streets.

Everything looked as if it had been dropped suddenly. The piles were scattered on the ground as if their owners had had run off or disappeared. But people didn't just disappear or run off without a reason. They ran because they were chased by something awful. .

We turned the corner to our street and almost stepped on a big frog. I froze and Jozlyn bumped into my back. The bats in my stomach were doing acrobatics.

"What—?" Jozlyn started to ask but lost her voice in surprise.

The frog hopped to the right and eyed us curiously.

"Ribbit!" it croaked in an authoritative voice. "Watch where you're going, peasants."

14

"Connor, is that you?" I squinted at the frog. It sure didn't look like Connor, all oily green and smooth. But it was big for a frog the same way Connor was big for a boy.

"It's me, peasant—Sir Connor," the frog exclaimed in an agitated croak. "The whole town's been turned into frogs, ribbit!"

While the frog didn't look like Connor, it sure sounded like him.

Jozlyn held up her hands. "All right, all right. I believe you." She glanced at me and I shrugged, then nodded in agreement. "We believe you. But where is everyone else? Have you seen our parents?"

Connor the frog flicked his long tongue out as he settled comfortably on his back legs. He seemed glad that we believed him.

"Everyone's gathered outside the mayor's house, ribbit,"
he croaked. "Even your parents. Mayor Garlo sent me to
scout for people. People-people. Not frog-people. You're
the first I've spotted, ribbit."

Jozlyn and I shared a quick look. "You don't know the
half of it," I told Connor in a rush. All the memories of the
morning's adventures came rushing back to me. "Cleogha
cornered us at the festival grounds. She tried to turn us into
frogs, too, but we hid in the woods."

Connor hopped closer to me. "In Everleaf Woods?
Ribbit. You're lucky then. Witch Cleogha got everyone
else."

Without any girly squeamishness, Jozlyn scooped Connor
into her hands. "Let's go see the mayor," she said sweetly
to Connor. "*Sir* frog."

Connor flicked his tongue again and let out a long, wet
raspberry. "Tttthhhbbttt! Very funny peasant, ribbit."

Jozlyn and I giggled. After the lonely trek through the
fog and the terrible scare from the witch, it was good to be
with a friend. Even a frog-friend.

I tried to enjoy the good feeling as we walked to the
mayor's house, but it didn't last. Everyone in town but
Jozlyn and me was a frog. I couldn't stay happy knowing
that.

Frogs and more frogs of every shape and size hunkered
and hopped outside the mayor's house. They croaked.

They shot their tongues at passing insects. They puffed and deflated their chins the way frogs do. Then they croaked some more.

Frogs sat on barrels and crates, in doorways and windows, along the edge of the road, and in the shade of buildings. It looked like the whole town of frog-people was there.

When they saw us, they quickly stopped what they were doing and became very quiet. The noise of their croaking and the slaps of their hopping echoed into silence.

I fidgeted nervously and Jozlyn stared hard at her feet. We might have been the tallest ones there but we still felt like children.

"Thank the lucky stars!" a frog suddenly shouted in Mom's voice. That broke the awkward silence and everyone sighed in relief.

Mom hopped eagerly toward Jozlyn and me. "I'm so happy to see you, ribbit. Your father and I were so worried when we discovered you missing this morning." Another bigger frog hopped alongside her. It was Dad.

"Mom! Dad!" Jozlyn wailed. She was crying, and I was close to doing the same. Seeing your parents as frogs would make anyone cry, I think.

Jozlyn carefully set Connor down and knelt on the ground so that she could embrace our parents. I sat down cross-legged next to her. Mom hopped onto my knee. Dad

bounced into Jozlyn's waiting hands.

We cried a little before a loud croak boomed out. "My, my, children. We're all relieved to see you, ribbit."

It was the mayor. He sat perched on top of a flat wagon without sides. Even in frog form, he still wore his usual top hat and had his bushy white mustache.

"As you can see," he continued, "we are in desperate need of your help."

I blinked and looked at Jozlyn. She appeared to be as surprised as me. "Us?" I asked. "How can we help?"

The witch had almost turned us into frogs, too. We'd barely escaped. I don't know what the mayor expected us to do.

Mayor Garlo puffed out his frog's chin. It reminded me of the way he huffed his cheeks when he was a person. His mustache stuck out straight and then fell slowly back into place.

"Why, to find the wizard, ribbit," he explained. "Wizard Ast will surely have the antidote to Cleogha's frog spell."

Mom ribbited suddenly. It sounded like a gasp.

Wizard Ast lived in a secluded tower on top of rocky Craggerscraw Hill. The tower was named Ninespire. Next to Croneswart Swamp, it was the last place I wanted to go.

The wizard wasn't mean exactly. He was more like grumpy and old and very much against surprise visitors. That's why he lived on the hill outside of town. He pre

68

ferred to keep to himself and not be bothered by regular townsfolk.

"Not my babies!" Mom croaked in alarm. I was nervous, too, and didn't like the idea of visiting the wizard uninvited, but why did she have to use the word *babies*?

The crowd of frogs started croaking and talking all at once. Some of them seemed to be in favor of sending Jozlyn and me to find the wizard. Others didn't.

"I say," a wrinkled old frog croaked, "the young lass should kiss us, ribbit. I hear that's supposed to break the spell."

The old frog sounded like Pa Gnobbles, the town's oldest living resident. He was over one hundred years old. By *lass*, he meant Jozlyn. Older folks called girls lasses and boys lads.

"Hush up, you old scoundrel," another frog croaked. This one sounded like Widow Marmelmaid. "Ribbit, listen to what the mayor has to say."

Everyone turned back to Mayor Garlo and quieted down.

"Who else is there to help us, ribbit?" croaked the mayor. He hopped to one side of the wagon and made a big show of peering about as if he was searching for something. Then he hopped to the other side and repeated the gesture.

"My, my," he continued. "I don't see any people but young Josh and Jozlyn. They'll have to make the trip. There's no one else, ribbit."

My heart sank but I had to agree. The sharp rocks of Craggerscraw Hill were too steep and high for frogs to climb. None of the townsfolk could make it up in frog form. That left the job to Jozlyn and me.

Jozlyn handed Dad to me and stood up. "We'll be honored to help the town in any way we can, Mayor Garlo," she said for both of us. Then she curtsied gracefully as if she'd been practicing. Even dressed in my clothes, she looked as elegant as a queen.

"No!" Mom cried from my lap. "Send someone else."

"My, my. Sara, Nigel, I'm sorry," Mayor Garlo apologized. Those were my parents' names, Sara and Nigel. "But there really is no one else, ribbit."

The mayor hopped from the wagon in a great leap and made his bounding way over to where Jozlyn and I sat with our parents. The crowd of frogs backed up respectfully to let him pass.

He stopped in front of us and puffed out his chin. "As Mayor of this town, ribbit, I hereby name you, Jozlyn and Josh, Official Wizard-Seekers of Tiller's Field. My, my. May you serve our town well."

Falling Uphill

15

Josh, Official Wizard-Seeker of Tiller's Field. It sounded like an important title, something a hero might be called.

I would have liked it if I hadn't known what it meant.

It meant that I had to climb Craggerscraw Hill, find a way into the magic tower, and convince Wizard Ast to help.

Any one of those would have been plenty of challenge, an adventure all by itself. Doing all three together was probably impossible.

Jozlyn looked ready to go and seemed to be enjoying her position as Official Wizard-Seeker of Tiller's Field. She stood in the center of a circle of croaking frogs who were congratulating her, thanking her, and wishing her luck on her heroic adventure.

She was a very brave girl, they told her. Please be careful and hurry back with the wizard.

No one enjoyed eating flies, it seemed. They would all appreciate us doing our best and being careful so long as we returned before dinner time.

Townsfolk crowded around me, too, but I wasn't paying much attention. I was thinking that one adventure a day was enough. Having a second one today didn't sound appealing.

I'd rescued Rosie, and Jozlyn and I had already escaped Cleogha. How much was a hero supposed to do in one day? On a breakfast of bread and cheese no less!

I was tired, nervous, and still didn't have a sword. Every hero should carry a sword no matter what Jozlyn said.

Pa Gnobbles got us on our way. "Back away now," he ordered the crowd. "The Wizard-Seekers have a job to do, ribbit. As soon as the lass collects her good luck kiss, that is." Even in frog form, he managed a cackle.

The townsfolk groaned at the suggestion. But to everyone's surprise, Jozlyn bent down and kissed the wrinkled old frog on the head.

Pa Gnobbles wheezed in delight.

"You're still a frog!" someone shouted at Pa. "The kiss didn't work."

"He's always been a frog," Widow Marmelmaid countered.

"More like a toad," someone else added. "Gives us good frogs a bad name." This got everyone laughing, even Pa

Gnobbles.

We said quick goodbyes from there. I don't think Mom would have allowed us to leave if we'd wasted much more time.

She kept telling us how proud she was of us. For some reason, she cried harder every time she said it. I guess being proud of your children can be depressing.

Connor hopped down the street with us but his frog legs couldn't keep up for long. When we turned north toward Craggerscraw Hill, he shouted "Good luck, peasants!" then turned back.

We rested a bit on the edge of town with our backs against a big oak tree. Craggerscraw Hill rose sharply in the distance. It stood alone in a wide green field that stretched as far as we could see.

The hill looked out of place, like a small mountain that had run away from its family. On top of the hill something sparkled in the sunlight.

It was Ninespire, Wizard Ast's tower.

I sighed heavily and got to my feet. "Might as well get going," I told Jozlyn, helping her up. "I'm sure we'll have more adventures waiting for us when we get back."

Jozlyn snorted. "You always wanted to have adventures. Quit whining." She gave me another pinch.

"I know, I know," I agreed. "But I still don't have a sword. A hero is supposed to have a sword."

I held up one finger. I wasn't about to let her interrupt, and I could tell she wanted to. Her mouth was already open. "And I don't want to hear another word about it," I snapped.

Jozlyn clamped her jaw shut tight and I started walking toward the lonely hill straight ahead. I felt a little better knowing I'd finally won one. But I'd have felt even better with a sword.

When we reached Craggerscraw Hill, it looked more imposing than ever. It was huge and made up of sharp rocks and sheer cliffs, and the hill was much taller than the trees in the Everleaf Woods. A narrow path looped its way up the side of the hill like the painted stripe on a top.

I leaned against a big flat-sided rock next to the path. "Are you sure you can do this?" I teased my sister. I was feeling much better about adventures again now that I had won an argument with her.

She scowled at me. "Race you to the—" she started to say, then took a look at the path. It was uneven and covered with loose stones.

"Never mind," she reconsidered. "We'd better take our time. Let's just make it to the top, all right?"

"Whatever you say," I said with a smirk. "You're my big sister. You'd know better than me."

Jozlyn sighed. "If that's how you want to be, Josh, fine. But you're still acting like a little kid."

She took a few steps up the path without me but suddenly turned around. "Heroes might carry swords, but little kids don't. That's why you don't have one."

With that, she began trudging uphill again.

I watched her go feeling sorry for myself. She was right. I was acting like a baby by pouting over a sword, and I was being mean to her for no reason.

I was acting like a brat. We had more important things to worry about, like getting to the top of the hill and saving our town.

When would I learn? Jozlyn wasn't that much older than I was, but she'd been behaving a whole lot more mature.

I scrambled up the slippery path as fast as I could. Jozlyn had already disappeared around the other side of the hill.

Rocks and dirt tumbled down beneath me and I slid backward. For every three steps I took, I stumbled down one or two.

When I rounded the first corner, I was surprised to find Jozlyn nowhere in sight. She was really moving fast. I needed to speed up or she'd be waiting at the top long before I arrived.

I'd never hear the end of that, especially after being such a brat.

I turned the second corner and still didn't see her. There was a big boulder in my way instead. It sat right in the middle of the path with no way around it. The boulder was shaped something like a giant egg and had a big crack running up and down its center.

"Jozlyn?" I whispered, suddenly afraid. There was no way that I'd passed her because the path was only wide enough for one. And there was no way around the boulder.

"Look, I'm sorry. I know I've been acting like a baby. Please don't play tricks right now."

I waited but heard nothing. There was nothing but me, the path, and the dead end.

A gust of wind ruffled my hair and made me feel dizzy. The ground was far below, and I wanted nothing more than to race back down the path.

Hoping to calm my nerves, I reached out and rested one hand on the big boulder. I kept picturing myself falling off the edge of the hill. It was a straight drop to the ground. A long, straight drop.

Crrrrench! The boulder trembled under my hand.

Shouting in alarm, I tumbled backward, tripped, and thudded onto my backside. Loose ground gave way beneath me and I started to slide down the trail.

Rocks poked and scraped me as I slipped helplessly. The walls of the path raced by and I clawed desperately at them to try to stop my descent.

Crrrrench! The boulder shook again and groaned. Dust swelled up around it in a cloud, and it seemed to grow larger.

Then I realized that the boulder was opening. The crack down its center was spreading, and the point at the top was splitting apart.

"Jozlyn!" I screamed. The boulder was alive and I was falling fast.

Floating, Flying, Falling

16

Above me, the boulder continued to split farther apart. It creaked and shook like a hatching egg. Its splitting halves looked like giant wings spreading open.

Sliding faster, I screamed. Falling from this height would mean certain death. But kicking my legs didn't slow me. Neither did grasping at the ground and rocks.

The rough walls of the path hurtled past me in a blur, and the path turned sharply just ahead of me. Rolling and slipping along with it, I tumbled down like an acorn bouncing through tangled tree branches.

My momentum flipped me onto my stomach and sent me zooming headfirst. The steep side of the hill sped closer. The field far below waited.

Helplessly, I watched it race nearer.

With the force of a punch, an unseen weight slammed

into my shoulders. It knocked the air from my lungs and propelled me faster along the slick path.

I was almost to the edge. I tried to suck in a breath but dirt and dust choked my mouth. I couldn't slow down. I was going to die.

As if watching it happen to someone else, I glided off the edge of the hill and into the air with a shower of debris. I soared into weightless silence.

I flailed my arms and legs but they touched nothing and felt nothing but wind. I was floating.

Flying.

Falling.

The ground raced up to meet me in a spiraling ocean of green.

I'd had dreams of falling before. Dreams so frightening that I woke gasping for breath. But those dreams were nothing compared to this sensation. This was real. This was the end.

The ground lurched and twisted, or maybe it was me.

Somehow I was turning. Not falling anymore. Wind howled in my ears and tore at my clothing. The hill rushed back into view. I was climbing higher!

Pain lanced into my shoulders again, and I realized that something had hold of me. It clutched me with sharp fingers of stone. I was almost sure that I was bleeding under its tight grip.

I turned to look over my shoulder at what held me. Wind brought tears to my eyes, but I made out the massive shape of a stone bird. It clutched my shoulders with granite talons.

Seeing it, I understood that the boulder on the path hadn't been a boulder at all. It had really been a giant bird made out of rock.

With its wings spread as we soared through the air, the great bird was as wide as a house. It looked like a statue come to life. Its powerful wings made a terrible grinding sound with every flap.

We climbed higher and the bird's chiseled beak let out a deafening rumble, sounding like an avalanche.

I risked a glance down and regretted it immediately. My stomach lurched at the sight, and I felt like I might pass out. Only squeezing my eyes shut as hard as I could stopped the awful sensations.

I wanted badly to stop wondering about how a rock managed to fly through the air. I wanted not to think about it, but I did anyway.

Rocks didn't fly, I knew. It was impossible. But here I was flying in the clutches of an enormous stone bird.

Maybe I was dreaming. Maybe I had already hit the ground. Or maybe the impossible wasn't so impossible …

Suddenly, I understood as if someone had shown me a picture. The reason the bird could fly was obvious. Especially considering where I was and whom I was near.

Wizard Ast.

The bird was a creature of the wizard's magic. With magic, I realized, the impossible was possible.

As we flew ever higher, I repeated that important lesson to myself. Hoping it was true and counting on it.

Magic makes the impossible possible. Magic makes the impossible possible.

I felt a bit safer as we soared through the sky, but I still kept my eyes closed.

Without warning, the pressure of the bird's powerful talons around my shoulders relaxed and I fell again. I opened my eyes and started to scream.

"Oof!" I grunted as my backside landed hard on the rocky ground. I think I might have fallen a whole two feet.

I opened my eyes to find Jozlyn standing nearby. She was rubbing her backside and staring at something behind me. I quickly jumped up to look in the same direction as her.

We were on top of Craggerscraw Hill. A black metal castle stood a short way off on a low rise.

The castle stretched high into the air and pulsed with an eerie blue light. Its base was shaped like a cylinder, but as it rose, it divided into an assortment of long arms like tree branches.

Some of the branches were higher than others, some

longer. Each arm ended in a unique tower of a different shape and size. One was long and thin, the next rounded at the bottom like a teardrop. Another was square.

There were nine towers in all. I didn't need to count them to know that. We'd reached the wizard's home, and now I knew the reason it was named Ninespire.

As if in confirmation, the rock bird that had carried me to the summit stretched its wings and shook its massive head. I hadn't realized the bird was so close. It had looked like a part of the hill.

In a deep, rumbling voice it said, "Welcome to Ninespire, travelers. My master is expecting you." Then it leaped into the sky and spiraled out of sight.

Choose Thou Wisely

17

As I gazed up at the castle, my heart sank. It was made up of many towers, not just one. Clearly no one from town had been up here in a long time. If they had, they'd never have called it a tower.

Ninespire was a wizard's castle.

The soft blue light pulsing from the castle bathed the ground around it in color. It pulsed like the heartbeat of a living creature.

"Josh, let's rest here a while, all right?" Jozlyn pleaded sleepily. Her face was dirty and there was a rip in the side of her tunic.

Still, Jozlyn had to look better than I did. New scrapes were added to the scratches from my dash through Everleaf Woods and from the silver-eared cat. A layer of dust coated my whole body, and the chalky taste of dirt was strong in my mouth.

"You got it," I mumbled drowsily. Resting sounded like a great idea. I could hardly keep my eyes open. "But not too long. Everyone in town is depending on us to hurry."

Of course Jozlyn knew that, but I was talking more to prevent myself from falling asleep than for any other reason. We were supposed to rest, not sleep.

I closed my eyes and waited for Jozlyn to respond. She didn't. She was asleep and I soon joined her.

I woke in the dark with a start. I'd been asleep for a long time and dreaming of falling. Jozlyn sat next to me. In the castle's soft glow, her face looked worried.

"Oh Josh, you wouldn't wake up!" she exclaimed. A tear rolled down her cheek. "I've been talking to you and shaking you forever."

I sat up quickly, feeling amazingly better. Still dirty and thirsty, but better. I patted Jozlyn's knee gently. "It's all right. I'm fine now. I'm sorry I scared you."

I was really making an effort to be more considerate of her feelings. After the way I'd acted at the bottom of the hill, it was important for me to make things right.

"Any idea how long we slept?" I asked.

"A long time," she answered. "We fell asleep in the afternoon and it's dark now. Everyone in town must be worried."

"And hungry," I added with a little grin. "Unless they ate

flies for dinner."

We smiled at that. I guess falling off a cliff and flying through the air in the talons of a rock bird can change your opinion of things. The townsfolk had to eat bugs until we returned, but they didn't have to have adventures.

Jozlyn stood up and tugged me to my feet. "Come on," she said, "there's something you need to see."

We headed toward Ninespire. Its blue radiance was the only light except for the stars overhead. We'd sure slept a long time.

"There," Jozlyn announced, pointing.

An enormous stone dragon statue stretched forward from the base of Ninespire. It wasn't a whole dragon exactly, just the upper half. It had a head, front arms, and chest. It sat the way a dog rests with its paws out in front of it and its head between them.

A flight of stairs ran along the dragon's back where ridges should be. Dragons always had rows of pointy ridges along their backs. The stairs ended at a set of large double doors in the side of the castle.

"Looks like the way in," I said hopefully.

"Sure Josh, think about it," Jozlyn said in her sister's voice. She'd obviously thought of something I hadn't. "How do we get up *to* the stairs?"

Good point, I thought, but didn't give her the satisfaction of knowing it.

The stairs started on the top of the dragon's head, about twenty feet above the ground. "Maybe we're supposed to climb up. Let's take a closer look."

As we approached the dragon, the ground started to quake and we both fell down. The dragon's eyes opened and shined with the same blue light as the castle behind it. Its mouth opened and it spoke in a deep voice.

"Three guesses thou art granted," it rumbled. I could feel the vibrations of the words rattling in my head. "Only one answer gives entry. All others, the fire of wrath. Choose thou wisely."

"What do you mean?" I called up to the dragon. But it wasn't paying attention to me or it didn't feel like answering. Instead it asked a riddle.

Soar through the air.
Breathe in the sea.
How can this happen?
How can this be?

Shrink to an ant.
Walk through a wall.
What is it to you?
What is it all?

Vanish from sight.
Turn ice to flame.
Tell me the secret.
Tell me the game.

"A game!" I shouted. "You're playing a game—"

"Wrong," the dragon rumbled. "Two guesses more. Choose thou wisely."

Jozlyn stomped on my foot. "Don't say anything it can hear," she hissed without moving her lips. "It'll think you're making another guess."

I exhaled in disgust and frustration. I'd wasted a guess with my outburst. Now we had only two left.

Two guesses more to answer the riddle or we'd face the dragon's fire.

Impossible Possible

18

Jozlyn grabbed my arm and led me away from the dragon. We walked far enough away so that we could talk without being heard.

"Fire, Josh. What do you think it means?" She looked worried again. She was playing with her hair, winding it around a finger.

"What do you think it means?" I repeated. I couldn't believe that she didn't understand. Sometimes she could be so smart but other times she acted just like a typical kid. "What do dragons breathe?"

She crossed her eyes at me. "Air," she huffed.

I almost groaned. Of course dragons breathed air, but that's not what I'd meant.

"Not in," I explained quickly. "What do they breathe out?"

Jozlyn's eyes widened in alarm. She'd finally gotten it. The dragon was going to breathe fire on us if we answered the riddle wrong three times.

"But how can someone do those things?" She meant the riddle. "Soar through the air. Breathe in the sea. The only time I've ever done them is asleep. You know, dreaming."

My head shot up and I smiled at her. "That's it, Jozlyn! The answer. It's dreams."

Her jaw dropped open and her eyes narrowed suspiciously. "Do you think it's that easy?"

"Why not?" I shrugged. "It makes sense, right? Go give it a try. We'll still have one more guess left if we're wrong."

She frowned at me and I knew immediately that I'd managed to say something that only a little brother would say. "We can't waste our guesses, Josh. We have to be right."

I folded my arms. What she said made sense, but we didn't have much choice. "Do you have any better ideas?" I asked.

She didn't, so we headed back to the dragon.

With her arms straight at her sides and her hands balled into fists, Jozlyn stood up tall in front of the dragon.

"Dreams," she said in a clear voice. She sounded confident and older than a teenaged sister.

The dragon wasn't impressed. "Wrong," it announced.

"One guess more. Choose thou wisely."

Jozlyn hung her head and started to shake quietly. But I didn't blame her. We'd both wanted the answer to be right so badly.

I'd been sure it was, too. A person could fly, turn invisible, and walk through walls in a dream. A person could do all the things named in the riddle.

But now we were out of ideas and almost out of guesses. What were we going to do?

We needed to get inside Ninespire. The wizard was in there and he had the antidote to Cleogha's frog spell. If we failed, everyone in Tiller's Field would be doomed to spend the rest of their lives as frogs.

I couldn't imagine our parents being oily green bug-eaters forever.

Away from the dragon, we flopped onto the ground. We were both exhausted again. Jozlyn was really twisting her finger in her hair now. The longer we sat there, the more she did it.

"I don't have any ideas, Josh," she told me, twirling her finger faster. Her hair was full of tangles. "I don't think the riddle is possible to solve. It must be some kind of—"

Possible. The word stood out to me like a solitary star in the night sky.

Excited, I jumped up. "You said it!" I cried, hopping about as if I'd been turned into a frog. "Possible! What makes something impossible possible?"

Jozlyn stared at me as if I were crazy. Maybe I was, but I knew the answer to the riddle just the same. I think that deserved a little craziness and hopping around.

My flight with the rock bird had taught me the answer to the dragon's riddle. I had thought it impossible for a rock to fly but the bird had proven me wrong. It could fly because of its special, secret power.

Magic.

Magic makes the impossible possible. Magic could certainly make someone capable of doing any of the things in the riddle.

I couldn't believe we hadn't thought of it sooner. We were stuck outside a wizard's castle after all. Who knew more about magic than a wizard?

I ran to the dragon without waiting for Jozlyn and skidded to a halt in front of it. Jozlyn didn't need to be standing next to me when I gave my answer. It was right. I knew it.

I pointed at the dragon defiantly. "Magic!" I hollered up at it. In response, the dragon opened its mouth and the red glow of a furnace roared out at me.

Metal Mayhem

19

With a terrified shout, I stumbled and fell back. In front of me, the dragon continued to slowly open its huge mouth. Heat blasted me and the red glow from inside was like blood.

The heat and light told me what would come next.

Dragon fire.

"Run!" I yelled to Jozlyn. She was somewhere behind me but not far enough. If she didn't hurry, she'd be caught in the coming fire right alongside me.

The dragon's mouth opened wider and the heat grew hotter.

I clawed my way to my feet, but my body didn't want to move. It hurt all over. My muscles ached and I was exhausted. I don't know how heroes manage to have adventures all the time. Didn't they get sleepy?

Jozlyn was at my side helping me to stand. I threw my hands against her shoulders and shoved with all the strength in my tired body.

"Run!" I yelled again, but she didn't budge.

"Josh, no," she said, stepping easily out of my weak grasp. "It's all right. You saved us." She pointed to the dragon behind me. "Magic was the right answer."

Still ready to run, I spun around. The dragon had opened its mouth all right, but not for the reason I'd thought.

Through the fiery glow, I saw that the dragon's tongue formed a stairway that climbed up through a hole in the top of the statue's head.

I exhaled loudly with relief. We were safe.

What a dope I was! When was I going to start thinking things through? I'd thought I'd learned that lesson after mistaking Sheriff Logan for a troll, but apparently not.

"It's all right, Josh," Jozlyn told me understandingly. "I almost made the same mistake."

Almost. She'd *almost* made the same mistake. That was some consolation. Almost making a mistake wasn't nearly as bad as making it for real.

If I kept making dumb mistakes, I'd never earn a sword or be a hero.

Jozlyn must have seen the sour look on my face because she grabbed my arm and roughly pulled me to face her.

"Look, you, stop feeling sorry for yourself," she said

seriously. She wasn't trying to sound like Mom or to be bossy. She was acting like an older sister with something really important to say. "If it wasn't for you, we'd be dead. The dragon would have breathed its fire on us. I didn't have the right answer. *You* did. Not me. You!"

She stomped off toward the dragon and stopped just outside its mouth. The red glow from inside mixed with the blue light emanating from the castle to bathe her in a shadowy purple.

"Do you understand?" she asked from over her shoulder. "Everyone makes mistakes and everyone lives with them. But not everyone answers a wizard's riddle correctly. Think about that."

With her arms folded, she tapped her foot dramatically. That meant I was supposed to get moving while I thought about what she'd said.

Together we walked timidly into the dragon's gaping mouth.

If I'd thought it was hot outside, I quickly learned a new meaning for the word inside the statue. The mouth was like an oven. Worse, an oven in a bonfire! We were both drenched in sweat before taking ten steps.

Maybe the dragon isn't going to breathe on us, I thought with a half-hearted smile. *Maybe it's going to roast us like holiday turkeys instead.*

Trying not to think about that, I took the stairs two at a

time. Jozlyn followed on my heels.

Gasping and fanning ourselves, we shot through the hole
in the dragon's head. Cool night air washed over us and we
felt better immediately. The stone stairs along the dragon's
back were warm under our feet but comfortable compared
to the temperature inside the mouth.

The double doors to the castle were closed when we
reached them. Made out of dark wood, they were deco-
rated with carvings and raised symbols. Stars, moons,
strange letters, and odd-looking creatures covered them.

If they were supposed to mean something, I didn't know
what it was. That was probably why I wasn't a wizard.

Jozlyn and I both shrugged at the symbols. "Think we
should knock?" I asked. The doors didn't have any
handles.

"That's the polite thing …" Jozlyn started but never
finished. She inhaled sharply and took a step back.

The doors swung silently inward to reveal a round room
lit brightly by torches on the walls. There was no one
inside, so we went in and the doors closed by themselves
with a soft click.

The round room reminded me of a museum. Colorful
paintings, gleaming weapons, and polished shields with
fancy crests hung on the walls. Sculptures of marble and
various metals lined the shelves of tall wooden display
cases. Banners and strange objects with wings dangled

from the ceiling.

Everywhere I looked I saw mysterious works of arts and ancient relics. Most of them I couldn't identify.

"Jozlyn, take a look at this," I called, peering curiously at a tangled heap of metal on the floor. It looked as if a display had collapsed on itself. The pile of objects blocked the way to a curved staircase that led farther up into the tower.

Other than the doors where we had entered, the stairs were the only exit.

As I approached the metal heap, it started to vibrate and tinkle musically. I threw an arm out to prevent Jozlyn from coming any closer. Musical or not, I didn't trust a moving pile of metal.

Rumbling now, the pile started to spin like a tornado. Metal pieces clanged loudly against one another and the whole pile floated up off the ground in a funnel.

The sound of scraping metal became deafening as the pile rotated faster. It screeched and shrieked, and I had to cover my ears.

"Look out!" Jozlyn screamed.

I dropped to the floor and rolled in time to see a painting hurtle through the air toward the spinning pile like a piece of metal toward a magnet. It crashed into the metal tornado and disappeared.

But the painting wasn't our only worry.

"Behind you!" I shouted, and Jozlyn dove to the floor. A flaming torch just missed smacking into her back. Like the painting, it flew directly into the whirling pile and disappeared in the confusion.

With our arms covering our heads, we watched more artifacts and artwork speed through the air and smash into the pile. They whizzed over our heads like arrows into a target. They came from all over the room.

Clang! went a sculpture.

Thunk! went another painting.

Cling! Clung! Glong! Things too fast or too small to see crashed into the pile.

Then everything stopped—the noise, the spinning, the objects racing through the air. There was only silence.

Jozlyn and I looked up, way up. In place of the pile, a tall metal creature stood in front of the stairs. It looked like a giant rusty skeleton. Torches burned where its eyes should have been.

Screeching like twisted metal, the creature reached for us with its enormous hands.

20

The metal giant scooped us up in hands the size of wheelbarrows. There was nothing we could do to stop it.

"*Whiz-click. M-M*-Master Ast will *s-s*-see you now," the giant stuttered in a metallic voice. It sounded like it needed a good oiling. But where, I didn't know. The skeleton didn't have a mouth that I could see.

It spun its metal head all the way around the way an owl does. Seeing it made my neck ache. I guess not having real bones will let you do things like that.

The creature carried us up the stairs, through a rounded stone arch, and down a long passage with many turns. I tried hard to pay attention to where we were going but the way became too confusing.

We were lugged through more doors carved with symbols, down long corridors lined with shining suits of armor, and up winding flights of tall stairs.

I couldn't have found my way out if I'd needed to. I could only guess that we were probably up very high in one of the castle's nine towers.

We passed through another set of wide double doors and the giant stopped. "*Biz-clack. Y-y*-your guests, Master," the creature buzzed in its mechanical stutter, and I turned my head to try to see in front of us.

"Put-set them down, Mephello, thank you," said a cheerful voice. "That will be all for now."

I assumed that Mephello was the giant's name. Funny, I hadn't thought of it having a name. It was just a monster to me.

Mephello plunked us down hard on our backsides and left the way we had come. Lucky for us the room was carpeted.

We looked around eagerly for the speaker. It had to be Wizard Ast.

I felt pretty good about myself right then, almost like a hero. We'd done all right for a couple of kids. The Wizard-Seekers had found the wizard.

We stood up tall and brushed ourselves off. Mephello hadn't hurt us, but he left a kind of rusty, dusty feeling on our skin.

In front of us stood a big desk cluttered with scrolls, parchment, books, ink pots, and feather quills. I suppose wizards did a lot of writing for their spells. A tall chair on the other side of the desk was turned away from us so that we couldn't see who was sitting in it.

I coughed nervously but Jozlyn spoke first. "Wizard Ast, sir, we hate to bother you." She glanced at me and swallowed, so I figured it was my turn to speak.

"We know you dislike visitors, sir, but …" I searched for the right words.

Suddenly, I felt edgy. I knew the wizard wasn't mean like Cleogha, but he still used magic. He could probably turn Jozlyn and me into frogs, too.

"Everyone in Tiller's Field has been turned into—" Jozlyn added but the wizard finished her sentence.

"Frogs," he croaked, his tall chair swinging slowly around. "Yes, I'm well aware of that, as you can see-tell."

His chair stopped turning. In it sat a frog with a long white beard wearing a pointed dark blue hat covered in lightning bolts and silver stars. It was a wizard's hat.

My knees trembled at the sight and what it meant. Wizard Ast had been turned into a frog!

Midnight Snack

21

"No!" Jozlyn exclaimed in shock and disbelief.

"You're a frog, too!" I gasped at the same time.

The frog-wizard croaked. "I'm afraid so, ribbit-croak."

My mouth hung open. I couldn't believe what I was seeing. Wizard Ast was a frog. That meant that Cleogha had beaten us here and that Ast probably couldn't use his magic.

Disappointment hit me like one of Jozlyn's sisterly punches. What were we going to do?

Our adventure was supposed to be over and we were supposed to be heroes. We'd made it up the hill, found our way inside the castle, and located the wizard. That was supposed to be the end of it for us.

I fell to the carpet and hung my head. Maybe we had to accept the fact that Cleogha had already won.

I felt miserable and hopeless. We had failed.

Jozlyn knelt down next to me. By the look on her face, I could tell she felt awful, too. She'd been putting on a good show of being brave and heroic but now she looked sad and tired.

Ast hopped up onto his desk. Papers scattered and an ink pot slipped off the edge to spill on the carpet.

"Squirmin' vermin worms!" he swore under his breath but still loud enough for us to hear. Then he quickly cleared his throat.

"Hmm, you weren't supposed-intended to hear that, ribbit-croak. Pardon-excuse me." Then he cackled long and loud. It was a happy sound, nothing like I expected to hear at a time like this.

He hopped from the desk to the floor in front of us. "There, there now, buck up children-young ones. Old Ast might be green but he still has a few tricks-surprises left. We'll teach that witch a thing or three yet, ribbit-croak." He winked mischievously, then added, "If it's the last hopping-leaping thing I do."

Like Pa Gnobbles back home, the wizard-frog was wrinkled with age. But his eyes were a piercing blue, very clear, and young looking. They didn't match the rest of his wrinkled body or his white beard.

Jozlyn glanced at him. "What do you mean 'we'll teach that witch a thing or three'? Do you mean 'we' as in you, me, and Josh?"

"Of course, of course! You, me, him, we. All four of us, ribbit-croak!" He cackled merrily. "Who else is there?"

Wonderful, I thought sarcastically. *Who else is there?* That was almost the same question that Mayor Garlo had asked right before he'd sent us off on our adventure to find the wizard.

Hearing it from Ast told me that he had a new adventure planned for Jozlyn and me.

"What is it we have to do?" I asked glumly. I wasn't exactly thrilled about running off to have another adventure. At least not so soon.

Ast hopped over to face me. His bright blue eyes seemed to stare right through me. "That eager-excited to get started, lad? That's the spirit, ribbit-croak! I'll make a hero of you yet."

I didn't have the heart to tell him that I'd been thinking I was already a hero just a few moments ago.

"For now," the frog-wizard went on, "let's fill your rumbling-growling bellies. The racket they're making is quite annoying, ribbit-croak. I can barely concentrate-focus on our cunning-clever plan with all that noise."

He leaped toward the doors. "Mephello!" he called, and the giant returned almost immediately with a loud clanging.

"Please be a good fellow-chap and see that our guests enjoy a hero's feast-meal." The wizard paused and tugged

104

on the end of his dangling beard with his webbed hand. "I do believe-think that jellypuff custard and snapsoda fizz are in order, ribbit-croak."

"Yes, please!" Jozlyn and I chimed together. We never ate jellypuff custard or snapsoda fizz except on special occasions.

This time we practically jumped into Mephello's big hands, and the big creature took us through another maze of passages, doors, and stairs. I didn't bother trying to remember the way.

"I'm going to eat four helpings of custard," I told Jozlyn excitedly, "and drink four mugs of fizz!"

She smirked at me from Mephello's other hand. "Well, then, I'll have five of each."

"Six!" I shouted back. I wasn't sure I could really eat that many helpings, but I couldn't be outdone by Jozlyn.

We continued our friendly competition until Mephello dropped us off in a small dining room. It had a long polished table with a fancy stuffed chair at each end. That was neat. Jozlyn and I sat at either end of the table pretending we were a king and queen.

Just as Ast had promised, there was plenty of custard and fizz. There was also warm bread, butter, mashed potatoes, crunchy green beans, roast beef, and gravy.

Even after all that, I still had room for two helpings of jellypuff custard. Jozlyn couldn't even finish one.

When we were done eating, Mephello took us to a big room with two huge beds covered by satin comforters and the fluffiest pillows I'd even seen.

There was clothing laid out on both beds. A cream-colored tunic and suede skirt with horses along the hem lay on Jozlyn's bed. A sleeveless black and green doublet with matching green hose waited on mine. The doublet had two bands of stamped swords running up and down the chest.

We figured the clothes were for us and were about to change when there came a weak knock on the door. I opened it to find Ast huffing and puffing on the other side.

"I do believe," he gasped, "that knocking on a door in frog form-shape is one of the most difficult-hardest things I've ever done." He panted for a few seconds then hopped into the room.

"The clothes and beds are for you," he explained, "but there's no need to change until morning-tomorrow, ribbit-croak. You have enough to think-worry about until then."

"Have you finished making your plan?" Jozlyn asked. She was holding the skirt with horses up against her waist and legs.

Her pose made me roll my eyes. She was acting just like a girl. Girls can be in the worst mood but if you mention new clothes, they get as sweet as jellypuff custard.

Ast hopped excitedly and let out a burping croak. "Why, yes! Yes, I have. And a very good plan-scheme it is." He hopped closer to the door and seemed ready to leave.

"But aren't you going to tell us what it is?" I demanded. I couldn't imagine getting to sleep without knowing.

"Oh, of course, ribbit-croak. How forgetful-absent-minded of me," he cackled happily. Then his penetrating blue eyes narrowed.

"The two of you will travel-journey to Croneswart Swamp to confront the witch," he croaked with a mysterious wink. "Now, goodnight and sleep-rest well."

With that, he bounded out the door and disappeared.

Gifts–Presents of Magic

22

I don't know about Jozlyn, but I hardly slept at all that night. A strange bed, the adventures of the day, and the thought of going to Croneswart Swamp were too much.

Surprisingly, Jozlyn and I didn't talk. We were too busy being nervous. Nobody in their right mind went to the swamp.

Nobody but a witch, that is.

After being kicked out of town by the mayor for flying her broom on Cauldron Cooker's Night, Cleogha must have fled to the swamp. It made a creepy kind of sense. A swamp, darkness, snakes and spiders—it seemed like the perfect place for a witch, if you asked me.

It was also the last place I wanted to go. Usually I like exploring but not in Croneswart Swamp. No one who wants to come out again goes there. Ogres and just about every other ugly kind of monster with a bad attitude were supposed to live in the swamp.

Thinking about it now, I gave Rosie a little squeeze inside my tunic. I felt guilty for hiding her from Jozlyn, but I could understand why my sister liked her so much. As long as Rosie was safe, so was I.

A loud knock on the bedroom door woke me. I couldn't believe I'd fallen asleep, but I really had to fight to pry open my eyes. They felt scratchy and heavy, and kept wanting to close.

Jozlyn was already awake and dressed in her new clothes. She opened the door.

Mephello stood on the other side. Without any sort of greeting, he scooped Jozlyn up with a big hand. Then his burning torch eyes turned to me.

I scrambled out of bed and put on my new green and black outfit. I hid on the far side of the bed so that I could move Rosie from my dusty old tunic to my new doublet without being seen.

As soon as I was done, I climbed into Mephello's open hand.

The metal giant carried us up stairway after stairway. We passed by a window once and I caught a quick glimpse outside. Far below I saw the rocky brown of Craggerscraw Hill and the green of the open fields beyond.

When we passed through a big trapdoor, sunlight stung

my eyes and I squinted against the brightness. A strong wind blew against my face.

Not only was I right about being *in* the tallest tower, now we were *on* it. I tried not to look down or to think about where we were. Jozlyn stared at her feet, clearly as uncomfortable as I.

Wizard Ast was there and so was one of the rock birds that had flown us up the hill the day before. The frog-wizard's long white beard whipped about in the wind. He squatted on top of a long wooden box.

"Good morning-noon, late sleepers!" Ast greeted us cheerfully. "Ready to begin your adventure, ribbit-croak?"

I almost laughed at that. *Begin* our adventure. What did he think we'd been doing?

"Ready and willing," Jozlyn spoke for both of us with a curtsy. I almost said something to her but shrugged instead.

"Wonderful-excellent!" exclaimed Ast. He hopped down from the box toward us. "Listen closely-carefully then. I have important-serious instructions for you."

Jozlyn and I knelt down to give the wizard our full attention. Anything was better than thinking about how far away the ground was.

"Now, my griffin will fly-carry you to the edge of Everleaf Woods," the wizard explained, pointing at the bulky bird behind him.

So that's what the rock bird was called, I thought. *A*

griffin.

"But the griffin cannot go any farther than the forest-woods," Ast went on. "It must keep my home-castle in view or it will lose its magic. Without magic, it cannot fly-move, ribbit-croak."

We both nodded and Ast continued his lecture. "From the edge-perimeter of the forest, you must walk west to the swamp. But do not …" He paused and raised one hand in warning.

"Do *not* enter-go in the mushroom patch. If you see even one mushroom, turn around and run-flee. The mushrooms near Croneswart Swamp are poisonous, ribbit-croak. You understand?"

We nodded again. This time with more enthusiasm. How far a griffin could fly wasn't nearly as interesting to us as poisonous mushrooms.

Jozlyn frowned and the wizard noticed right away. "Do not despair-fear, lass," he told her excitedly. "Mighty green Ast has gifts-presents of magic to share."

He cast a glance at the short box he'd been sitting on moments earlier. Then he looked at me. "Go on, lad, open-unlock it, ribbit-croak."

Half of me wanted to tear open the box as if it was a gift-wrapped birthday present. The other half wanted to push it over the edge of the tower.

Magic could make griffins fly but it could also turn a

town of people into frogs. Whatever was in the box could be dangerous.

I swallowed hard as I pulled off the lid. Tucked snugly inside the box were two wondrous items. The first was a slender, metal wand. It pulsed with purple light that rolled up and down its length like a wave.

The second made me forget the wand. It was a sword, a marvelous sword like I'd never seen before.

The blade of the sword was slender but strong and plenty sharp. Its hand guard was polished and made of twisting metal bars that spiraled around the leather-bound hilt like a spider web. I'd never seen anything so handsome and deadly.

"A rapier, lad," Ast croaked from behind me. "Not as heavy as other swords, but fast, ribbit-croak. Perfect for a young man-lad."

Jozlyn gasped from over my shoulder. I hadn't even heard her approach. The rapier had had my full attention.

Jozlyn pointed at the glowing purple wand with a trembling finger. "Beautiful," she whispered without actually touching her gift.

Ast cackled happily. It was a nice sound, the kind of laughter you know is *with* you, not *at* you.

"Take them, ribbit-croak," he said between chuckles. "They are for you. Use-wield them well-wisely."

I reached for the rapier slowly. I couldn't believe it was

for me. After all of my wishing and complaining, I finally had my own sword just like a real hero.

Drawing the graceful weapon out of the box, I stood and turned around without taking my eyes from the rapier. The height of the tower and the gusting wind didn't bother me just then.

A feeling of nervous excitement warmed my chest. I was Josh, Official Wizard-Seeker of Tiller's Field.

Josh, Adventuring Hero.

Josh, Sword-Bearer.

I felt stronger, braver, and older with the rapier in my hand. I could face any danger with my new blade.

"Now then," the wizard-frog said, "let's get you two off to Everleaf Woods and on the way-path to Croneswart Swamp, ribbit-croak."

My good feeling faded when I remembered where we were going and why Ast had given us such fantastic gifts. Cleogha the witch was waiting for us.

Zippin' Griffin

23

Ast hopped over to the griffin. The great bird hadn't moved since we'd arrived. Except for the fact that its eyes scanned the horizon back and forth without blinking, I would have thought it was asleep.

"Down," the wizard croaked, and the bird responded by crouching low to the roof of the tower and stretching out one wing at an angle.

The tip of its wing touched the roof to create a kind of ramp up to its back. A big saddle perched there, waiting for us, along with a knapsack of food.

Jozlyn understood what we were supposed to do first. With her new purple wand in hand, she nimbly scaled the griffin's wing and plopped herself into the saddle. She gripped a set of reins dangling from the bird's stone beak.

"I get to steer," she announced to me with a quick wink.

I smirked at her but didn't say anything. Having her steer was fine. It meant that she would have to keep her eyes open during the upcoming flight. That was something I wasn't sure I wanted to do.

I sheathed my rapier and climbed up after her.

"Wait-hold on, ribbit-croak!" Ast called urgently. "You must use-wield the wand against the witch. Speak-say the magic word *grizt* to make it work. Concentrate on a frog and she will be turned-changed into one. That will break-counter her spell over the rest of us, ribbit-croak."

Jozlyn nodded her head vigorously. *"Griznt!"* she shouted. "I won't forget."

Just in case she did, I repeated the mystical word silently. *Griznt, griznt.* I didn't want to take any chances.

The griffin lurched suddenly beneath us and spread its wings.

"Good luck!" Ast croaked loudly, hopping backward to give the bird room. "And stay clear-beware of the mush-room patch!"

Then we were off. In a jerking gait, the griffin charged toward the edge of the tower. Just as we were about to plummet off the side, the bird jumped and flapped its mighty wings.

I held my breath. The griffin's jump hadn't gotten us very high. The edge of the tower rushed past and we fell straight down.

Jozlyn shrieked and then so did the griffin. It was a piercing cry and not very reassuring. The bird's whole body trembled with the sound.

I couldn't shriek myself but I wanted to. My stomach was in my throat as if it refused to fall with the rest of me.

"Griznt!" was all I managed to gasp through my clenched teeth. Maybe the griffin needed a boost of magic to get safely airborne.

At the last possible moment, the griffin turned up hard, and we skimmed safely over the summit of Craggerscraw Hill like a crane in search of fish above the waters of a lake. The ground dropped away, and we soared into the open sky above the grassy plains.

Our flight didn't last more than a quarter of an hour. Probably less. But I'll never forget it for as long as I live.

I can't believe I'd wanted to keep my eyes closed! This flight was nothing like being dragged by the shoulders again.

I couldn't take in the sights fast enough. I kept swinging my head from side to side, trying to see everything at once—the approaching forest, clouds, Tiller's Field, farmhouses, and flocks of startled birds.

If a witch ever turned me into something, I decided right then that I hoped it would be a bird.

Jozlyn kept pointing and shouting "Look!" and "Over there!" I'm sure she was having as much fun as I was.

The ride ended too soon. Banking sharply to the right, the griffin spiraled down and quickly came to a gentle landing. Then it crouched again and stretched out one wing toward the ground.

Jozlyn and I reluctantly climbed out of the saddle. We hadn't wanted the flight to end. We both knew that we might never have the opportunity to ride a griffin again.

We also knew that the dangerous part of our new adventure would begin as soon as we set foot in the forest.

I retrieved a knapsack full of food from the griffin's saddle and then the great bird leaped into the air and soared rapidly out of sight.

We were alone again. I patted the rapier belted to my hip for reassurance and saw that Jozlyn clutched the glowing wand in her fist.

"Griznt," I said to her, forcing a smile. My stomach was back where it belonged after the zooming flight and now it was doing somersaults.

I glanced at the woods and a shiver slithered up my back. "Let's go," I said quietly.

Big Double Trouble

24

Everleaf Woods rose up before us like a tangled green wall. Its trees and foliage seemed thicker and even less friendly here than near the festival grounds.

Jozlyn swallowed hard and stared up at the trees. "Keep that sword handy," she told me quietly. "And remember, *pointy end goes in the troll.*"

I almost smiled at Jozlyn's joke, but then she stepped into the woods and disappeared. I hoisted the knapsack over my shoulder and hurried to catch up.

Less than twenty feet into the woods, we lost all sight of the sun overhead. It was as if the trees were telling us that we were on our own.

There wouldn't be a friendly wizard waiting to help us when we reached our destination this time. There would be a nasty witch looking to turn us into frogs.

Even if you are dead before I do!

Cleogha's words came back to me as we carefully picked a path through the trees. I couldn't control a shudder but thankfully Jozlyn didn't notice.

For long, tedious hours we crept through the forest. Every so often we checked for moss on the trees and headed to the left from it. To the west, just like the wizard had told us to do.

With every step, the trees seemed to crowd closer together. Twisted roots stuck up from the ground like bony fingers trying to catch our feet and trip us. Strange birds that we never saw clearly cried out and flapped their wings loudly overhead. Their movements rustled the leaves and branches all around.

Once, we even heard a heavy crash and the sharp sound of snapping branches. The noises echoed for a long time afterward.

Hearing them, we crouched beneath a tangle of bushy ferns and counted to one hundred, then to a thousand. But we didn't hear anything else. Even the birds had gone silent.

We headed west again. Dark-spotted white trees started to appear more frequently.

"Look, birch trees," I pointed out to Jozlyn. I knew from the trees near Gurgleburp Creek that birches often grew near water. I lowered my voice. "We must be getting close to the swamp."

I think Jozlyn wanted to respond but she started coughing instead. She waved her hand at me to keep going and nodded. She'd noticed the trees, too.

When I started coughing a few minutes later, I knew that something was seriously wrong.

I glanced back to see Jozlyn on her knees coughing hard. I couldn't see her face. She had her head down, and her long hair hung in front of her.

I also noticed hundreds of mushrooms surrounding her. She knelt in a cluster of rust-colored stems, and a wispy orange cloud floated up around her head.

"Mushrooms!" I cried. Wizard Ast had warned us about the poisonous mushrooms, but we'd been too busy looking for moss on the tree trunks to pay attention to the ground.

"Get up, Jozlyn!" I shouted again and again as I ran to her side. But soon I was coughing too hard to say anything more.

I grabbed Jozlyn under the arms and hauled her to her feet.

"Back," she gasped between coughs, waving her arms toward the way we'd come.

I agreed without question. Even though we were getting closer to the swamp, we couldn't make it through the mushrooms. We had to turn around and look for a different path around the dangerous fungus patch.

Turning to run, my foot came down in the middle of another orange cluster and a dusty cloud puffed up into the air. It floated around my head like smoke and sent me into another fit of coughing.

As I struggled for breath, the orange dust slowly settled on the ground. Wherever it landed, new mushrooms popped up from the soil.

Pop-pop popop-pop! Mushroom after mushroom sprouted up from the forest's dark floor.

"Run!" I screamed, shoving Jozlyn in the back to get her moving.

Coughing so hard that tears streamed down our cheeks, we stumbled back the way we'd come. We leaned against one another for support, and I had my arm around Jozlyn's shoulder.

Thud!

The heavy crash we'd heard earlier boomed again. This time it came from somewhere ahead of us.

We were trapped and couldn't turn back. The air around us was just starting to clear, and we were finally catching our breath.

Thud! The crash came once more, closer and louder.

I looked up to see the biggest creature I'd ever seen.

It stood taller than a man with another man on his shoulders. It had dark brown skin covered with short black hair and a body of enormous, bulging muscles.

The creature had two arms and two legs, but its face was flat and its bottom jaw stuck way out. Two yellow-stained tusks protruded from its long bottom jaw. It clutched a big sack in its hand and wore a club on its belt.

It's probably looking to bring home a bag of children for dinner, I thought glumly.

I recognized the creature from Dad's stories. I was sure it was an ogre. I could see it clearly. And any second, it would see us, too.

Jozlyn and I turned at the same time. We knew what had to be done. Choking dust or not, the ogre was bigger trouble than mushrooms.

We fled back into the mushroom patch as fast as our feet would carry us.

25

We held our breath and sprinted ahead deeper into the mushroom patch. Orange mushrooms sent up their poisonous clouds. New mushrooms *pop-popped* to life all around us.

The ogre had spotted us and was chasing hard. We could hear and feel the thunderous crashing of its heavy feet. No matter how fast we ran, the thumping of the ogre didn't get any quieter. It rattled our teeth and the branches of nearby trees.

The ogre was really, really big!

"Don' run, leedle peeples," it called to us in a slow, slobbery voice. It sounded sleepy or as if it was already chewing on a crunchy dinner of children.

Funny, Dad's stories never mentioned the fact that ogres could talk.

The trees ahead thinned out and we were running through thick yellow clouds, not orange like before. They swirled like dust from a shaken rug.

"What's—?" I heard Jozlyn gasp in surprise as she stared at the ground.

I looked down to see that the floor of the forest was covered with mushrooms. More than we'd ever seen before. They covered the ground like a thick carpet. They even grew on the trunks of trees.

But these mushrooms were bright yellow, not dull orange. They were different than the ones that had choked us.

Jozlyn slowed and pointed to a short hill ahead. "We can hide up there," she said, still gulping for breath.

The yellow mushroom clouds didn't make us cough. I guess we were past the danger and it was all right to breathe.

"I'll use the wand if the ogre gets too close," Jozlyn added.

The ogre's booming steps didn't seem to be slowing. Using the wand was probably going to be our only option. We weren't having any luck outrunning the monster.

"Hurry!" I said, drawing my rapier. It made the same metallic *shing* sound that Sheriff Logan's sword had made when he'd drawn it on Cleogha's snake. The sound made me feel a little better.

"Coom back, coom back!" the ogre shouted in its sloppy

speech. It was almost on top of us. Knowing that made me run faster.

Jozlyn's eyes widened and she let out a little squeal. She grabbed my arm and hauled me uphill.

The hill's incline was steeper than it looked. When we reached the top and threw ourselves onto the ground, we were both panting loudly. Yellow mushrooms puffed their clouds and filled our every breath.

"I'm so tired," Jozlyn whispered almost too quietly for me to hear.

"I know," I agreed but couldn't bring myself to say more. My arm ached and my rapier felt heavier than I remembered. Hadn't Ast promised that it was light enough for a boy to use?

I fumbled with it clumsily and stuck it back into its scabbard. Even so, I could still feel its dreadful weight pulling my hand to the ground.

I glanced at Jozlyn. She was lying on her back with her eyes closed. She held the wand in both hands against her chest and didn't move. I couldn't even tell if she was breathing. She looked dead, like a corpse arranged for burial.

A mushroom puffed right in front of me and its dust tickled my nose. I tried to cover my face but my hands and arms wouldn't respond fast enough. I felt as if I was wearing wet clothes filled with sand.

Stay clear-beware of the mushroom patch. Wizard Ast's croaked warning came back to me, and I suddenly understood what was happening. The yellow mushrooms weren't choking us the way the orange ones had, but they were just as dangerous.

They were putting us to sleep in the middle of Everleaf Woods.

I struggled to roll over and sit up but my arms and legs wouldn't work. They tingled painfully as if I'd been sitting on them for too long.

"Jozlyn …" I mumbled, "have to … wake …"

"Leedle peeples," came the ogre's call again. This time the wet voice was much closer than it had been.

My eyelids drooped closed and I was powerless to stop them. I'd never felt so sleepy before. It took several seconds or maybe even minutes for me to force them open again.

When I did, I wished I hadn't.

The ogre's flat, big-jawed face stared down at me. The monster might have been grinning, but I couldn't be sure. A thick strand of drool trickled out of its mouth and spattered its dingy tan tunic.

"Hallo, leedle bite-shized peeples," it gurgled at me.

I tried to say something but couldn't make a sound. My eyes closed again and I saw only darkness.

A Short Climb to Nowhere

26

Worms. I'd been dreaming of worms. I started, trying to wake.

My eyes still didn't want to open. They felt sticky and wet as if I'd been asleep too long or crying.

I rubbed them to get them to cooperate, imagining that I could still smell the scent of moist soil from my dream.

Rolling onto my side, I peered blearily about. An uneven dirt wall peppered with rocks and fuzzy roots loomed next to me.

Wherever I was, it wasn't on the hill where Jozlyn and I had fallen asleep. I was somewhere underground, probably in a cave. The ogre must have—

The ogre!

I bolted to a sitting position and quickly patted my doublet and hip. With relief, I felt them both, Rosie and my rapier. But where was Jozlyn?

I squinted across the cave in the dim light coming from a wide tunnel behind me. My eyes were still having trouble focusing. There was a slender lump of something huddled against the far wall. When I saw that it wasn't moving, I inched closer.

The lump was Jozlyn in the same corpse's position that I'd seen her in on the hill. Her hands were folded across her chest with the glowing wand between them. She still didn't seem to breathe.

In alarm, I scurried closer for a better look and leaned my head down toward her chest. I wanted to listen for a heart-beat.

"Oh no you don't!" Jozlyn said suddenly, sounding like a person scolding a puppy. "The wand is mine. You got the sword, hero-boy."

With a flick of her wrist, she swatted me on the nose with the wand. My nose started to tingle the way it had after the silver-eared cat had scratched it.

I sat back up and tried to think of something clever to say, but couldn't. When I really want to be funny or to sound smart, my mind draws a blank. Later, like when I'm lying in bed at night, that's when I think of the right thing to say. Hours too late.

Jozlyn waved the wand in small circles just inches from my tingling nose. "Gri …" she teased. "Gri …"

"Jozlyn, no!" I shouted in a whisper. The last thing I wanted was for her to experiment on me with the wand. She was close to saying the magic word *griznt*.

"Gri … griffin!" she finished with a giggle, shaking the wand vigorously in my direction.

"Come on, be serious," I told her angrily. "The ogre must be nearby. How else do you think we got here?"

I stretched out my arm to indicate the cave and realized this was a switch. I was bossing Jozlyn around and sounding like Mom or Dad.

She shrugged at me and pouted. "We're still alive," she said, sniffing. Then her eyes brightened. "Maybe someone rescued us from the ogre!"

I liked the idea right away but didn't think it was very likely. How many people could live near Croneswart Swamp—a witch, an ogre, and some heroic rescuer? That didn't even take into consideration all the creepy-crawlies.

Plus why would a rescuer take us to a cave like this?

"I don't—" I started to say but Jozlyn was already moving.

"Let's find out," she said, taking charge and being the big sister again. In a crouch, she headed toward the tunnel leading out of the cave. I followed on her heels.

The tunnel widened so that we could walk side-by-side. It was tall enough for us to stand, too, but we crouched anyway. Crouching just seemed like the thing to do while sneaking along.

Flickering light guided us down the tunnel. I was pretty sure it was from a torch or fireplace. The air got warmer the farther we went and the reddish glow got brighter.

The tunnel opened into another cave. We crouched near the entrance on opposite sides of the tunnel and studied the room. It was round and had a large opening in the ceiling toward the far side. Through the opening, I could see daylight, trees, and leaves.

A big wooden ladder leaned against the wall next to the opening, and a fire burned inside a ring of large stones. The smoke from the fire wafted up through the opening in the ceiling.

There was no one in the cave. But by the size of the ladder, I had an idea of who might live there, or what. No one but an ogre needed a ladder that big.

O-gre, I mouthed silently to Jozlyn. Now that we knew where we were, talking out loud didn't seem like a good idea.

I pointed to the ladder and Jozlyn nodded.

Still crouching, we scampered to the ladder as quickly as we could. We had no idea when the ogre might return so we had to hurry. This might be our only chance to escape.

I cupped my hands at knee level to give Jozlyn a boost and she started to scramble up the ladder.

Pushing and pulling one another, we slowly climbed. For

some reason, the climb made me think of a baby trying to get out of its crib. To the ogre, we probably were baby-sized.

Halfway up, we heard a familiar thump, and then a big shadow darkened the opening above.

The force of the thump shook the ladder, knocking us down to the rung below. We landed on our backsides and wrapped our legs around the wood.

When I caught my balance, I risked a look up. Sure enough, the ogre peered down at us with a big, sloppy grin on its face.

"Hallo, leedle peeples," it slobbered.

Jozlyn gasped and lost her grip on the wand. It tumbled and bounced down the ladder. The fall seemed to last forever, and then the wand landed right in the ogre's fire.

Rude Dinner Guests

27

As Jozlyn's wand fell, something happened to me. It was like figuring out the answer to a riddle. One moment I had no idea and the next I couldn't believe that I hadn't seen the answer before.

I knew what I had to do.

I pulled myself up and jumped back down to the ground with a grunt. Even before hitting the ground, I ripped my rapier from its scabbard and stared defiantly up at the ogre.

From the ladder, Jozlyn shouted. "No, Josh! What are you—?"

I didn't pay her any attention. I pointed my rapier at the ogre and worked up my deepest voice.

"Leave us alone!" I screamed at the monster. "We aren't food and we won't be your dinner!"

The ogre stared back at me with a blank look on its face,

so I continued. "You have to let us out of here right now. We're on an important mission to Croneswart Swamp."

The ogre squinted at me and scratched its head with a stubby finger. "Leedle peeples … dinner?" it asked slowly as if it were trying to figure out a riddle of its own.

"No, no," I replied, wagging the point of my rapier back and forth and shaking my head. "Not dinner."

A gaping smile split the ogre's face and it let out a deep, bubbly laugh. It clapped its meaty hands together. "Leedle peeples needs eatin'. Mougi feeds mushrooms."

The situation wasn't going at all like I'd thought it would. Instead of being frightened by my threats, the ogre seemed happy, maybe even delighted.

I lowered the point of my rapier in confusion. What was happening here? Was the ogre named Mougi? Did it want to feed us poison mushrooms?

Jozlyn hopped down from the ladder and rested an arm on my shoulder. "He's not going to hurt us, Josh," she told me softly.

He? She was calling the ogre a he? It was a monster, a beast from a story. An *it*, not a *he*.

I pushed Jozlyn's arm away and took a step forward. I wanted the ogre to know that Jozlyn and I did not agree. She might climb into a cooking pot, but I wouldn't.

"Stand back, beast," I ordered. The seriousness of my tone surprised even me. "We're leaving." I started to turn

134

to Jozlyn.

Before I turned all the way around, there came a heavy thud followed by something very big and very solid crashing against my side.

I went sprawling helplessly to the dirt floor, and the air burst from my lungs. My rapier flew from my hand and clattered noisily against the stones near the fire.

"Bad and rudely manners," the ogre gurgled unhappily.

The creature was almost on top of me. I could feel the rumbling vibrations of its words in my chest.

Still gasping, I rolled onto my side and looked up. The ogre stood over me with its hands on its hips. It must have jumped through the opening above when I'd turned my back.

Without my rapier, I was defenseless, and Jozlyn's wand was still in the fire.

Book By its Cover

28

"What are you going to do to us?" I asked the ogre. I didn't mean for it to happen but my voice squeaked. It didn't sound very heroic.

The ogre stared at me for a long time. A strand of drool streamed from its lips, forming a small puddle on the floor. Finally, it wiped a hand over its mouth and smiled again.

Surprisingly it didn't have any teeth except the two front tusks. That fact should have told me something, but I wasn't thinking straight. I was more worried about being eaten, and I remembered Dad's stories.

"Mougi feeds yous then takes yous away from mushrooms," the ogre told us. Its tone was friendly and its words didn't sound threatening. "Mushrooms make bad air for short leedle peeples. Mougi carries yous to swamp."

"So you … you're not going to eat us?" I stammered.

Jozlyn's foot found my shin with a quick kick less than a second later.

Mougi wheezed and coughed once. The sound reminded me of a dog's bark.

"Eats you?" A second barking cough turned into a wet laugh. "Eats? Mougi eats mushrooms, not leedle peeples. Mougi gots no teef." The ogre smiled broadly to display its toothless mouth.

Jozlyn giggled but covered her mouth politely. She obviously wasn't afraid, and her confidence told me that I'd jumped to the wrong conclusion again.

When I saw an ogre, I immediately thought of a man-eating monster. But Mougi wasn't like that. He wasn't an *it* after all.

He was a vegetarian.

"We thank you, Sir Mougi, for your kindness," Jozlyn said with a curtsy. "My name is Jozlyn and this is my little brother Josh. We would be grateful for your help."

When she'd said *little brother*, she'd glared at me, making a point. I was the younger one who had acted without thinking again.

"Me Mougi," the ogre beamed, thumping his wide chest with a thumb as thick as my arm. "Nice very much to meets you leedle peeples."

He bent over and picked up my rapier and Jozlyn's wand from the fire. The flames didn't seem to bother him at all.

137

"Yous sticks," he said seriously.

Sticks! To the ogre, my sword was nothing but a harmless stick. What in the world had convinced me to draw it in the first place?

I grumbled to myself and accepted the ogre's offer. Jozlyn took her wand and curtsied again. The wand didn't look like it had been damaged by the fire. It glowed as brightly as ever.

But I did wonder about it and decided to try something later.

"We go now," Mougi rumbled. "Yous climb on and we leave. We munch yummy mushrooms while Mougi walks."

Jozlyn looked to me and I shrugged, so we scrambled onto the ogre's back. His legs and arms were like tree trunks, making the climb easy. Mougi then scaled the ladder as if he had wings instead of two children on his back.

I decided that it was a good idea to remember how strong ogres were in case I ever met a mean one with teeth.

Beyond the cave, we found ourselves on the top of a steep hill. Mushrooms of every color blanketed the ground as far as we could see—red, blue, silver, brown, pink, and lots of other colors. They looked like a meadow of brilliant flowers.

As the ogre made his thumping way down the hill and through the forest, mushrooms everywhere erupted in colorful dust clouds. But none floated up any higher than the ogre's waist.

That's why Mougi was unaffected by the mushroom patch. He was tall enough to be safe. Sitting on his shoulders, so were we.

"Mougi, how do you eat the mushrooms?" Jozlyn asked as she bounced on the ogre's shoulder.

The ogre chuckled. "Mougi pops 'em in 'is mouth an' swallows. No needing for to chew."

We laughed at that. The toothless, vegetarian ogre had to be one of the strangest inhabitants of the forest.

With snakes, goblins, spiders, and maybe even a troll or two lurking about, who would have thought that we would meet such an unusual ogre?

"But Mougi," Jozlyn went on, "the mushrooms are poisonous. Don't you get sick eating them?"

The ogre stopped and held his belly in a great laugh. "Mougi no eats the bad dust," he said as if it were the easiest thing to figure out. "Here, yous watch."

Mougi studied the ground a moment then picked a big, dusty red mushroom. Careful not to raise it too high, he slapped the mushroom gently against his thigh. Dark red dust wafted into the air and slowly settled back to the ground with the familiar popping of new mushrooms.

"Eats it," Mougi encouraged, handing the mushroom to Jozlyn.

The mushroom was as big as her hand, and she took a timid bite. Her reaction to it reminded me of the night we'd eaten at Wizard Ast's castle.

"Josh, try some!" she exclaimed without offering me any of *her* mushroom. She took another bite and juice dribbled down her chin.

I was about to grumble when Mougi handed me a speckled golden mushroom.

Not bothering to experiment with only a nibble, I took a huge bite. If mushrooms were good enough for Jozlyn, they were good enough for me.

I wasn't disappointed.

"Warm honeybread with cinnamon!" I exclaimed, letting them know what I'd tasted.

"Gooey raspberry dumpling," Jozlyn cheered.

"Mmm, goblin liver stew," Mougi burped on a black-striped green mushroom. Jozlyn and I scrunched up our faces in disgust. We wouldn't be eating any of those.

Then another thought occurred to me. Some mushrooms were poisonous and would kill me if I ate them. It wouldn't be smart to eat *any* mushroom without an ogre around, or a parent.

For the next hour or so, Mougi continued to carry us deeper into the forest. The whole way, we feasted on mushrooms.

White-dotted blue ones tasted like chilled blueberries

sprinkled with sugar. Light tan with brown swirls tasted like griddle cakes covered with maple syrup.

The tastes and varieties were amazing. We even washed down our meal with silver-white mushrooms that tasted just like snapsoda fizz.

When Mougi stopped, it took me a while to realize that we'd left the mushroom patch behind. Before us, moss-covered trees with tangled vines and black blossoms grew in twisted shapes like stooped skeletons. Patches of fog swirled through their twisted branches and over the damp ground.

"Croneswart Swamp," Mougi said clearly and quietly.

As if to confirm Mougi's announcement and welcome us, a big black snake slithered over a log and disappeared into the fog.

Grizni

29

"Mougi stops here," the ogre told us sadly. He must have been concentrating because his usual slobbering was at a minimum. "Mougi no leaves mushrooms for long. Utters come an' fall to sleeping or worse."

I understood. Mougi had to protect those who wandered into his mushroom patch. It was his home and he felt responsible for its wondrous but dangerous magic.

We said our goodbyes quickly and then watched him lumber out of sight. When we couldn't hear his thumping steps anymore, we turned back to face the swamp.

The scratch on my nose started to tingle again and I brushed at it in irritation.

"Jozlyn, I've been thinking about something," I admitted hesitantly. I didn't think she would like my idea.

"Oh no," she started to criticize, but an odd blue and

orange spider scuttled up a nearby tree and seeing it put her out of the lecturing mood.

"Well," I started slowly. "It might be smart to test the wand. You know, to see if it still works after falling into Mougi's fire."

I didn't want to mention that we would probably get only one chance to use the wand. If Jozlyn missed Cleogha or did something wrong, we would be doomed. She *had* to turn the witch into a frog on the first shot.

Jozlyn looked at me and then at the wand. She twisted a strand of hair with her finger. "You're right," she said. "What should we try it on?"

Amazed, my mind drew a blank. I hadn't thought she'd agree. Testing the wand was too much like playing.

"How about a tree?" I finally offered. It seemed like a good suggestion. There were plenty around and she could hardly miss.

She considered this for a bit then shook her head. "A tree is alive. If we go around changing living things into frogs, how are we any better than Cleogha?"

I hadn't thought of that.

"Here," Jozlyn pointed with her foot, "this log. It's a tree but already dead."

I took a step back to give her room to work.

Jozlyn raised the wand and aimed down her arm at the log. She took a deep breath and then whispered, *"Griznt."*

Nothing happened.

She shook the wand. *"Griznt,"* she repeated, this time more loudly. Still nothing happened.

She waved the wand back and forth. She rotated it in a circle. *"Griznt, griznt, griznt."*

Nothing, nothing, and more nothing.

"Maybe you're not—" I started to suggest, but Jozlyn cut me short.

"Do you think you can do any better?" she asked in frustration. "Here." She pushed the wand at me and it poked me in the chest.

That's when my whole world changed.

A thunderous boom exploded in my head, and a blinding purple spark flashed between the wand and me. Then I was flying backward through the air. I crashed into a tree and landed in a coiled heap.

The next thing I knew I was looking up from the ground at Jozlyn's concerned face. Her blue eyes were wet and a tear streamed down her cheek. I wasn't sure why but she looked so much taller than usual.

"Jozssslyn, ssss," I hissed. "What happened, ssss?"

30

"Change me back, ssss!" I hissed again as my tongue flickered in and out of my mouth. "I don't want to be a ssssnake."

Tears streaked Jozlyn's face. "I'm sorry! I'm trying," she cried. "I don't know how to change you back." She gripped the wand so tightly that her knuckles turned white.

"Try ssssomething! Just do what you did again but backward."

My nose tingled and I licked it with my tongue. Doing so made me think of the way Cleogha's broom-snake had licked her. Yuck! "Pleasssse hurry."

Jozlyn collapsed into a sitting position and threw her arms up into the air. "Give me a second! If I'm not careful, I'll turn you into the first thing I think of again."

The first thing I think of.

145

That was the answer.

"Jozssslyn, what were you thinking about jusssst before you changed me?"

She snapped her fingers and smiled through her tears. "A snake! That's it. I was thinking about that creepy snake we saw on the log."

"Great, now we're getting ssssomewhere." I slithered closer and propped my head on her foot. Slipping across the wet ground on my belly felt nice, like having someone scratch my back. "Now think about Jossssh and change me back, ssss."

Jozlyn jumped to her feet. She pointed the glowing wand at me and raised her other arm, but then a mischievous look twinkled in her eyes. A crooked smile tugged at her lips.

"Green-haired Josh with fangs?" she teased, staring at me with a raised eyebrow.

"Yessss, very funny, ssss," I hissed. My tongue flicked anxiously.

"Or maybe two-year-old Josh in swaddling clothes?" she giggled. She was having too much fun at my expense.

"Jusssst get on with it or I'll bite you!" I threatened.

Jozlyn closed her eyes in concentration. I waited nervously and twitched my tail back and forth.

"Griznt," she said when she opened her eyes and bent over to touch the wand to my head.

I felt warm and cold all at once. Purple light flashed

146

before my eyes, and I squeezed them shut against it. Even with them closed, I could still see and feel it as if I'd stared at a purple fire.

When it faded, I opened my eyes and realized that I was lying on my stomach in the dirt. I had my arms flattened along my sides and my legs pressed together. My tongue was sticking out of my mouth.

Afraid I looked silly, I scrambled to my feet in a hurry and brushed myself off. To my surprise, Jozlyn wasn't laughing.

She pulled me into a tight hug. "I'm so sorry," she wailed into my ear. "It must have been awful for you."

I shrugged and patted her back gently. I'd been expecting more teasing. "It's all right now. You fixed it," I told her reassuringly.

I had wanted to yell at her for changing me into a snake, but it didn't seem right now. She hadn't meant to do it. Plus, I was the one who'd encouraged her to test the wand.

Still, I couldn't help hissing into her ear one more time.

She swatted me lightly on the head with the hand that wasn't holding the wand. "Next time you might not be so lucky, snake-boy," she smiled, but her happy look vanished in a hurry.

We both looked around. "Now that we're in the swamp, where do we go?" Jozlyn asked, almost whispering.

Swampland crowded all around us. Hulking trees and

vined plants grew close together in snarled clusters as if they didn't have room to spread out. Fog swirled about in streaming patches like ghostly tentacles.

Whenever I turned my head to the right, my nose started to tingle. "Mean cat," I mumbled after feeling the strange itch for a third time. Would the scratch ever heal?

"What do you mean?" Jozlyn asked.

I waved my hand. "Nothing. Just remembering that cat from the festival, is all."

I didn't want to talk about it. There was something odd and mysterious about that cat. Black cats were supposed to be bad luck, and I was sure that included black cats with one silver ear that ran off with pixie dolls.

"Come on, let's go this way," I suggested, pointing to our left. I didn't want anything to do with an itchy nose or with going to the right.

Our progress through Croneswart Swamp was slow. Logs, roots, and pools of murky water appeared in our path every few steps and we were often forced to climb over or go around obstacles.

Pretty soon, our new outfits from Wizard Ast were torn and spattered with globs of sticky mud. The swampy muck covered our hands and faces and even clung to our hair.

Exhausted, we stopped at the edge of a dirty lagoon. The water was dark and smelled like dead fish rotting on the shore.

The lagoon covered a large area and we couldn't see the other side. The water disappeared in a thick bank of fog.

Jozlyn sat down on a big brown rock and let out a long sigh. "We're lost," she moaned. "There's no way across that lagoon. Unless …"

She looked up at me suddenly. The mischievous look was back in her eyes. Before I could ask what she had planned, she pulled out her wand and squatted in front of the rock.

"Griznt," she said with surprising authority. Then she tapped the rock with the glowing tip of the wand.

I turned my head and squinted, expecting the brilliant purple light again. Instead, the rock glowed softly and started to melt. Then it slid off the edge of the shore and disappeared into the murky water.

The lagoon bubbled once, then went still.

"What did you do?" I asked. I hadn't expected my sister to melt rocks. That wasn't going to get us across the lagoon.

"I don't …" she started to say, then excitedly pointed out into the lagoon. "Look!"

Something was swimming toward us, something big with a long, skinny neck. The creature came all the way up to the shore and slapped two big fins down at our feet.

It was a turtle, the biggest I'd ever seen. It was pale green with a tan-striped brown shell.

The turtle's neck extended and its oblong head dipped in

149

a bow. "Master Gramble, Turtlecraft Extraordinaire, humbly at your service," it said in a deep voice.

Crooning in Croneswart

31

Leaning close to Jozlyn, I whispered into her ear so that the turtle couldn't hear me. "A turtle? Couldn't you think of anything better? A boat, maybe, or a raft?"

I paused for a smirk. "A big log?"

"He'll do just fine," Jozlyn snapped defensively and plenty loud enough for Gramble to hear.

Great, I grumbled silently. *Now I'll have to ride across a swamp on the back of a turtle that knows I'd rather be in a boat.* The idea didn't make me feel confident about the trip.

"You'll carry us across the lagoon, won't you, Master Gramble?" Jozlyn asked, patting the turtle on its head.

"It will be a sincere honor and pleasure to bear you to any destination, near or far," the turtle responded in a slow drawl. Every word and syllable was pronounced precisely,

151

and he paused between sentences.

In other words, it took him a long time to say anything.

"Please climb aboard and we shall depart at once," he instructed.

Gramble was big, almost five feet wide. There was plenty of room on his shell for Jozlyn and me.

"Should we just … step on you?" I murmured awkwardly. It was an odd question.

"Aye, if you please, young sir," Gramble replied.

Trying to hold back grins, we carefully stepped onto the turtle. The situation was just a bit silly, and we both wanted to giggle. Who ever heard of heroes riding off to vanquish a witch on the back of a turtle?

True to his word, Gramble didn't seem to mind us standing on his shell, and in almost no time, we were bobbing far out in the lagoon. I turned around to check but couldn't see the shore behind us. Like the far shore, it was lost in the fog.

"Please, good travelers, do instruct me as to our destination," Gramble requested after we'd gotten underway. He sure had a formal way of speaking.

"To the witch's lair, Master Turtle," Jozlyn requested, mimicking Gramble's speech.

We both assumed that Gramble would know the way to Cleogha's lair. He lived in the swamp near her. That made them neighbors.

"Hmm, hmm," Gramble drawled. "I am afraid that I do not know the way, my lady. I have seen a witch only once. She actually placed her vile foot upon me, but I know not where to find her now."

Jozlyn frowned and looked to me for a suggestion.

Gramble was really a rock, not a turtle, I realized. Rocks didn't get up and move around by themselves. But maybe he'd seen something or someone that would give us a clue.

"Gramble, uh, sir," I asked, trying to sound formal, "have you seen anyone else, or maybe heard anything unusual recently?"

That wasn't exactly what I'd wanted to ask, but I couldn't come up with a polite way of asking, *We know you're usually just a rock, but can't you be more helpful?* If I'd have asked that, I was sure I would have ended up in the lagoon.

"Well," the turtle said, "when the witch stepped on me, a cat was with her. It was an odd black cat with one silver ear."

Jozlyn and I looked at each other in surprise. That silver-eared cat sure had a knack for showing up in strange places. Thinking about it, I started to get an idea.

"The cat was her pet then?" I asked.

Gramble didn't respond right away. He seemed to be thinking. His head tilted this way and that.

"Nay, sir," he finally said. "I do not believe the cat and

153

witch were in cahoots. Nor do I believe the cat was the witch's familiar."

It took me a minute to translate that. Gramble meant the witch and cat weren't friends and that the cat wasn't the witch's pet. Witches and wizards often have magical pets called familiars.

"In fact," Gramble went on, "I am confident in asserting that the witch and cat were most certainly enemies. The cat was hissing vehemently at the witch."

I smiled at Jozlyn who scrunched her eyebrows together in thought. I could tell that she was putting the pieces together the same way I had.

"So the cat—" she said, thinking aloud.

"—has been trying to help us," I finished.

At the festival, the silver-eared cat had taken Rosie, probably to get us to follow it. Then it had gone to town and tried to get Sheriff Logan's attention.

If those things were true, then the itch on my nose must mean something, too. But why did it tingle only at certain times?

I had an idea and snapped my fingers. "Master Gramble, please stop swimming for a moment. Just float while I try something."

The turtle stopped paddling, and we drifted to a slow halt. We rocked gently in place like a swimmer treading water.

Concentrating on my nose, I turned in a slow circle. I

154

spun around three times. Sure enough, I felt the tingling itch whenever I faced my right.

Satisfied, I said, "To the right, Gramble. The witch lives to the right."

I winked at Jozlyn and tapped my nose. If the cat really had been trying to help us, the most important thing it could have done was tell us where to find the witch. The tingling in my nose, I figured, was the cat's map to the witch.

"*Starboard*, sir," Gramble corrected. "When on the water, right is starboard." With that, the turtle turned to face the correct direction and started paddling again.

Starboard and port. I'd heard those before but hadn't ever had reason to use them. On a boat, *starboard* meant right and *port* meant left. I'm not sure why, but that's what sailors called them.

We continued for quite some time. Every so often I asked Gramble to stop so that I could get a fresh direction for the tingle on my nose. Then we made an adjustment to our course and got on our way again.

I couldn't be sure if we were making good time because I didn't know how far we had to go, but at least I was sure we were headed the right way.

"My feet hurt," Jozlyn complained, fidgeting.

Mine did too, I realized. It was hard standing in one spot for a long time. I kept shifting my weight from foot to foot.

Gramble cleared his throat to get our attention. "If I may

be so bold as to suggest a song to pass the time? Rocks are renowned for their pleasant voices and for knowing many things."

"Please, Sir Gramble! That would be lovely," Jozlyn exclaimed.

I couldn't help but agree. We were getting close to the witch now. Anything to get Cleogha and my sore feet off my mind would be appreciated.

"Ah, very good, then," Gramble said, clearing his throat once more. Then he began his song.

> From the dark and the damp
> Of Croneswart Swamp,
> I've a tale to tell.
> Listen up, listen close,
> It's a joyful romp.
> One I know quite well.
>
> Sing high, sing low—
> Sing out, don't you know.
> Hey you, hey me,
> Sing out joyfully.
>
> Raise your voice, sing along,
> And gather near.
> Climb aboard my shell.
> Say goodbye, wave your hand,
> We're leaving here
> To swim 'round a spell.

Sing high, sing low—
Sing out, don't you know.
Hey you, hey me,
Sing out joyfully.

Through the fog and the mist,
We'll travel far.
Anywhere you name.
Close your eyes, make a wish,
Think of a star.
Dream high, that's our aim.

Sing high, sing low—
Sing out, don't you know.
Hey you, hey me,
Sing out joyfully.

For a few minutes, Jozlyn and I forgot all about being on a dangerous adventure and having sore feet. We even forgot about witches and cats and frogs.

We tapped our feet to Gramble's song and hummed along to the catchy tune. In no time, we were singing the chorus with him.

When the last notes drifted off into the silence of the fog, Gramble spoke. "It seems, hmm, that we have arrived."

I glanced up. A jagged shoreline appeared out of the mist straight ahead, and a creature paced along the water's edge. Its black paws stepped gingerly on the damp ground.

I should have expected the silver-eared cat to be waiting for us.

From Mud to Beast

32

With my rapier held tightly in my hand, I followed Jozlyn
onto shore.

The cat watched us cautiously from a few feet away. Its
back was arched and the fur on its tail was puffed up and
sticking straight out. Its silver ear twitched.

Jozlyn pulled out her wand and started toward the cat.
She had a determined look on her face. "Where's my doll,
cat?" she scowled. "Where's Rosie?"

Oh no, I thought. Jozlyn didn't know that I had Rosie
tucked inside my doublet. I wondered if I should show the
doll to her.

Before I made my decision, the ground exploded. Dirt
and rocks shot into the air. Twigs, mud, and leaves pelted
my face and rained down on my head.

From everywhere, slimy mud-creatures rose up from the

ground. They were made of the dead things lying about the swamp—vines, deadwood, mud, and leaves. Some were short and wide, others tall and thin. But all of them came right at Jozlyn and me.

Without doubt, I knew they were some sort of witch's creation.

One reached Jozlyn and its crooked fingers clawed toward her face.

"Griznt!" she roared in a voice I'd never heard her use before. Then she slammed the wand like a club against the mud-creature's forearm.

Purple light exploded, surrounding the creature. When it faded, the mud-beast was gone and a brilliant monarch butterfly fluttered daintily nearby.

"Nice one!" I shouted encouragingly, and meant it. I honestly didn't think I'd ever felt so proud of my sister. But I couldn't enjoy the feeling long because a mud-creature swatted at me with its gooey arm.

Without thinking, I brought up my rapier to block the creature's attack. The muddy arm was aimed at my face. I deflected the blow and sent it over my head.

Then the most amazing thing happened. My rapier burst into flame.

Silvery fire ignited along the length of the blade with a roaring *whoosh*. I cried out in alarm until I realized my hand was perfectly safe.

159

My rapier was magic!

I gripped the flaming sword in both hands and swung it back and forth. The advancing mud-creatures stopped. Some even cowered.

"Stay back," I yelled, waving the rapier. Its fire hissed like an angry serpent.

In the corner of my eye, I saw Jozlyn fall. A pack of mud-creatures surrounded her. They were slowly forcing her back toward the lagoon. Then her heel caught against a root just as she shouted, *"Griznt!"*

She landed in the mud with a wet squish and the wand tumbled from her fingers. She clawed after it but the mud-beasts were closing too fast.

"Nooooo!" I screamed, thrusting with my rapier once more. The silvery flames brushed against the nearest mud-creature. In a blink, the beast melted into a pulpy mass.

I saw my chance then. Jozlyn needed me.

Holding my sword like a lance, I charged the mud-creature to my left. My blade connected with its thigh, and the flames worked their magic. The beast collapsed like a glob of hot wax.

As if in slow motion, I watched another mud-beast snatch up Jozlyn's wand. The creature raised its arm and prepared to swing down.

It was going to use the wand on her! It was going to turn her into something horrible that only a mud-creature could

imagine!

I screamed again, louder and full of anger. Then I dove forward with my rapier straight in front of me.

The fiery blade caught the wand just as the mud-beast brought down its arm. When the two magical weapons clashed, a violent explosion and deafening crash thundered through the swamp.

Purple light and silvery fire erupted in a hissing geyser. The wand shattered into fine, sparkling dust, and the flames on my rapier flickered and died.

True Enemy

33

The explosion burst outward like the ripples in the water after a boulder drops into a pond. A piercing noise filled my ears, and blast of wind knocked me to the ground.

The witch's mud-creatures stumbled about blindly. They bumped into trees and each other. Some even splashed woodenly into the lagoon.

All the while, they sagged and fell apart, melting like snowmen caught in the rain. The ground swallowed them, and they quickly vanished.

The magic all around me was coming apart. Even the silver-eared cat mewed and clawed at the red collar about its neck. As I watched, it dropped to its stomach, twitched, and went still.

I would have felt sorry for it had I not heard Jozlyn groan. She lay inches away. Her face was covered with mud and her new tunic was torn and dirty.

She weakly pushed herself up on her elbows and fluttered her eyes open. "What happened?" she asked breathlessly.

"The wand exploded," I whispered, "I think … I think destroying it destroyed all of the nearby magic. The mud-creatures fell apart. Even the cat—"

Jozlyn cut me off and sat all the way up with a start. "What's Cleogha doing here?" She pointed at something behind me.

I turned to see Cleogha lying in the mud where the black cat with the one silver ear had been moments before. Her long hair was streaked with silver and she wore her black outfit with the red trim.

I gasped with understanding and threw my hand to the scratch on my nose. Cleogha's silver-streaked hair and red-trimmed outfit were too much like the cat to be a coincidence.

My mind put the last piece of a puzzle into place.

The silver-eared cat and Cleogha were the same! Cleogha had been the cat all along. The cat had been Cleogha. When the wand had exploded and destroyed the nearby magic, it had changed Cleogha from the cat into a person.

"The cat!" I explained quickly to Jozlyn, my words rushing out of my mouth. I couldn't believe that Cleogha had been the cat all this time. "The cat *was* Cleogha. But the wand changed her back."

Jozlyn nodded slowly. The pieces in her puzzle were fitting together, too.

"But, Josh, if Cleogha was the cat, who turned everyone into frogs?" she asked. "Remember, we saw the cat on Trooping Fairy Day. The day *before* the frogs."

I stared at Cleogha's unmoving body. Maybe she hadn't been our enemy after all. But if not her, then who?

From the fog ahead, a harsh voice cackled evilly, slowly, and softly like dried leaves swirling in a breeze.

"*Eh-heh-heh-heh.* Figure it out yet, fools?" the voice taunted.

A woman stepped from the mist. She was tall, old, very skinny, and had a long crooked nose. If someone had asked me to draw an ugly witch, my drawing would have looked exactly like her.

Like Cleogha, she wore a witch's costume—a pointed hat, curl-toed shoes, and a long dress. But her outfit was dark blue with orange trim, not black with red like Cleogha's.

The new witch leaned heavily against a blackened broom as if it were a walking stick and bowed her head slightly.

"I am Witch Zeila, children," she sneered, "your true enemy. You have been chasing the ghosts and phantoms of the wrong witch."

She cackled again and I shuddered. Somehow Zeila's laugh sounded even more terrifying than Cleogha's. In fact, everything about her was more terrifying.

I knew immediately that this woman would never have been allowed to live on the edge of Tiller's Field selling troll charms the way Cleogha had.

Witch Zeila pointed at Cleogha's body with the end of her broom. "I appreciate you ridding me of that one," she said arrogantly. "For that, welcome to Croneswart Swamp. Now you pests are mine."

Eight-Legged Prison

34

Witch Zeila lifted her long bony arms. She muttered to herself then raised her voice in a short spell:

> Rustle rowdy, stir and groan.
> Whisper wicked, curse and moan.
>
> Awake, awake from your bed.
> Arise, arise, now, living dead!

Suddenly the vines and branches near Jozlyn and me began to move. They slithered like snakes through the mud. They crawled over us, twisted around our hands, and pinned our arms behind our backs. Before we could react, we were tied and trapped.

The mud-creatures came to life again, too. Sticks, mud, and vines sloshed and slapped together, reforming the beasts. Half a dozen of them stood up and shambled into a ring around us.

One of the mud-beasts stepped on my rapier and ground it into the mud. As I watched its silvery hilt disappear, my hope for escape went with it.

"What to do?" Zeila wondered aloud, tapping her pointy chin. "You see," she admitted, "I used up my frog magic on your pathetic town and during our meeting on the edge of the woods yesterday."

Yesterday? I thought in disbelief. Had it only been one day since Jozlyn and I had gone in search of Rosie? It hardly seemed possible. So much had happened.

Zeila cackled again and shrugged. "No matter. I will think of something particularly nasty. You deserve it for the trouble you've caused me."

With a quick flick of her wrist, she commanded her mud-creatures to haul me and Jozlyn to our feet. Then the creatures poked us in the back with their sharp, pointy fingers. It was their way of telling us to move.

We didn't argue. We'd lost the rapier, destroyed the wand, and our hands were tied. There was nothing we could do but march exactly where the mud-beasts pushed and prodded us.

Oddly, something tickled my stomach, but with my hands tied, I couldn't do anything about it. I tried to ignore the feeling as much as possible.

A short time later we climbed a tall, oblong hill and

stopped. It was bare of the gnarled trees and plants that grew elsewhere in the swamp.

At the top, Zeila strode to the front of our small group and held her broom above her head. In a loud voice, she shouted a sentence or two of harsh words that I couldn't understand. One of them sounded like *griznt* but I couldn't be sure.

Lowering her broom, the witch turned back to us and smiled smugly.

Behind her, something moved. It appeared out of the trees at the bottom of the hill. At first I thought it was a giant insect, but then it staggered closer. It was a small wooden hut built on eight spider-like legs.

The hut shuddered and creaked and stalked up the hill like a predatory cat through tall grass.

I tried not to react but the hut was amazing. In ten great strides, it scaled the hill and came to a stop. Its jointed legs bent and lowered the hut to the ground.

Jozlyn let out a soft whistle that only I heard. We'd seen all kinds of magic in the last two days, but the hut still surprised us. Was there nothing magic could not do? How could we hope to defeat it?

The mud-creatures prodded us again, so we didn't have more time to gawk.

The inside of the hut was much larger than I expected, but we weren't allowed to look around there either. Zeila led us to a small storage room and closed the door without saying a word.

From the other side of the door, we heard a heavy bolt turn and tumble. We were prisoners.

Rosie is Real

35

I sank to the floor and Jozlyn did the same. We said nothing for a long time. We just sat there feeling sorry for ourselves.

At first a small open window gave me a tiny bit of hope, but I quickly realized that it was too small for Jozlyn or me to wiggle through.

I hung my head and rested my chin on my chest, and the tickle on my stomach came again. I was too busy sulking to pay any attention to it.

"Don't give up," Jozlyn squeaked in a high-pitched whisper. At least I thought it was Jozlyn. But when I looked at her, she had her head down, too.

"Did you say something?" I asked her.

She tried to smile but didn't seem to have the energy. "No, I thought you did."

The tickle inside my doublet hit me again, and I couldn't control a giggle. It made me wiggle and squirm so much that I ended up tipping over onto my side.

When I thumped onto the floor, the tiny voice squeaked again. "Aha!" Then the tickle wiggled across my stomach, over my chest, and up onto my collarbone.

Rosie suddenly popped out of my doublet and flitted into the air. She hovered on her delicate wings inches from my face.

"Hi, Josh-a-bear," she chirped. *Josh-a-bear* was a nickname Mom called me. She was the only one who had ever used it before.

From the other side of the room, Jozlyn gasped. "Rosie!" she sobbed and scrambled across the floor.

Rosie twirled in the air like a dancer. Her little pink dress spun about her legs. "Jozlyn!" she exclaimed, flying to embrace my sister. Her tiny arms hugged Jozlyn's cheek.

"I thought you were lost," Jozlyn cried. "Where have you been?"

Rosie zipped backward to look Jozlyn in the eye. "Josh will explain everything later when the time is right. Right now, I must leave. My magic will not last long."

She glanced up at the window overhead then back to Jozlyn. "You will see me again, my Jozlyn, but only as I was before. I will not be able to call upon the magic of the broken wand again."

Rosie fluttered toward the window then returned to hover near Jozlyn's face. "I love you with my whole heart," she squeaked, kissing my sister on the nose.

Then Rosie turned to me. With one hand on her slender hip, she winked. "And you're pretty cute, too, Josh-a-bear."

She twirled a final time and then disappeared through the window.

"I love you, too," Jozlyn whispered as tears streamed over her smiling cheeks.

Vanquished

36

"I told you Rosie was magic," Jozlyn reminded me confidently. Despite having her hands tied and being a prisoner of Witch Zeila, she smirked.

In my mind, I rolled my eyes, but I wasn't about to disagree. Doing so would only start a fight. Rosie had magic because we'd broken the wand, not because she was a real pixie.

But Jozlyn wouldn't admit the difference, and I guess it didn't matter. Rosie had come to life and was trying to rescue us. That was what counted.

"Now scoot over here and turn around," Jozlyn said. "Let's get our hands untied."

I smiled to myself. That was the take-charge big sister I knew. Seeing Rosie had really boosted Jozlyn's spirits. I knew Rosie had boosted mine. We could hope again, at least a little.

Sitting and leaning against each other's back, Jozlyn and I fumbled with the vines around our wrists. I'd tug and wiggle hers until my fingers ached, and then Jozlyn would take a turn at mine.

The small room was dim and full of shadows when the binds on my hands finally came loose. I stretched my arms and wiggled my wrists. They felt cramped and sore, but a whole lot better now that they were free.

I quickly finished untying Jozlyn's hands.

She massaged her wrists and frowned. "Rosie's been gone a long time. We might have to escape on our own."

I hadn't wanted to say it, but I'd been thinking the same thing. Rosie had vanished through the window hours earlier, sometime in the afternoon. I feared that the magic of the wand hadn't lasted long enough for her to come back with help.

I tried to rub some feeling back into my wrists. "We can't fit through the window," I said, "and the door is locked. Got any ideas?"

Even in the faint light coming through the window, I saw Jozlyn's eyes narrow. "We fight," she said with determination. "I'm tired of being afraid, Josh. I'm tired of hiding and I'm tired of witches." She threw up her arms. "And we don't even know this Witch Zeila!"

I was about to respond when the door suddenly burst open

in a shower of splinters. There wasn't even a click from the lock. The door just flew back and smacked into the wall as if it'd been kicked by someone as big as an ogre. The impact shook the whole hut.

"I smell a fairy!" Zeila roared from the doorway. Her wrinkled face was red with rage. "Where is the winged rodent?"

Jozlyn was on her feet and had her hands balled into fists at her sides. I could tell that she was about to do something brave, or something stupid.

Then again, when an angry witch was in the room, maybe brave and stupid were the same thing.

"We don't know what you're talking about," Jozlyn lied. "What's a fairy smell like anyway? Not as bad as a witch, I hope."

Zeila hissed in fury and her whole body quivered. "Insolent brat!" she screeched. She raised her broom and pointed the handle at Jozlyn.

With a clap of thunder, Jozlyn flew across the room and landed against the wall with a thud. Her arms and legs were pressed flat against the wall as if she was lying on a floor with something heavy on top of her. It was obvious that she couldn't move.

Then Zeila turned her dark eyes to me.

In that moment, I thought of my parents and how they'd been turned into frogs. I thought of my friend Connor, of

Wizard Ast and Sheriff Logan, and even silly old Pa Gnobbles. Everyone in Tiller's Field. They believed that Jozlyn and I could save them. They were depending on it. They were depending on us.

I thought of them all and I wasn't afraid anymore. Screaming, I ran at the witch with my arms out to tackle her.

One second my feet were pounding across the floor and the next they were spinning in the air, touching nothing. I was floating helplessly like a leaf caught in the wind.

Zeila threw back her head and howled savagely. "What now, little ones?" she taunted. *"Eh-heh-heh-OW!"*

Something crashed into the back of her head. It was Rosie. But not Rose the living fairy, Rosie the pixie doll.

Cleogha charged into the room after Rosie. She clutched my muddy rapier in one hand. Her black witch's outfit was filthy and twigs dangled from her dirty hair.

Just as I'd hoped to do, she ran into Zeila and they both went down in a snarling heap. My rapier clattered to the floor.

I guess tackling a witch is a smart move after all.

Cleogha's appearance shocked me and my mind whirled with questions. *What is she doing here? How is she alive? And most importantly, Is she on our side?*

Then Zeila lost hold of her broom and the air suspending me above the floor seemed to melt. I floated down like a feather.

Behind me, Jozlyn gasped for breath. "The broom!" she panted hoarsely. "It's the source of Zeila's magic!"

I knew immediately that she was right.

When Zeila had dropped the broom, her magical hold on Jozlyn and me had failed. Somehow, the witch's spells were tied to her broom. Without it, Zeila couldn't keep her spells working.

That meant that if we destroyed the broom …

I didn't have time to finish the thought. I ran across the room and jumped over the wrestling witches.

They continued to tear and claw at each other like wild dogs. But even for Cleogha's size advantage, it didn't look like she could hold out much longer. Zeila had a fistful of her hair and was struggling to stand.

I snatched my rapier from the floor where Cleogha had dropped it. As I turned, Zeila shrieked. "What are you doing?"

I froze and Zeila laughed. Cleogha lay motionless at her feet. "Put the sword down, little boy," she commanded.

My heartbeat pounded thunderously in my ears and time seemed to stop.

Thump. Zeila stepped toward me. *Thump.* She raised her arms. *Thump.* She sucked in a deep breath. *Thum—*

"Now, Josh!" Jozlyn shouted, and time screamed to a start. She was on her knees with Zeila's broom clutched in her outstretched hands.

I looked at Zeila and raised my rapier. "What am I doing?" I mocked, and Zeila seemed to shrink, becoming small and weak. Her eyes were wide with terror. "I'm vanquishing you!"

My rapier came down swiftly and sliced through the long handle of the broom in Jozlyn's hands. Colors and lights exploded, and a gust of wind blasted me off my feet.

Zeila's cry of "Nooo!" was the last thing I remembered.

Apprentice Rewards

37

It was over and we were home, the heroes of Tiller's Field. Only we didn't feel much like heroes. We mostly felt tired.

We'd arrived home late on the shoulders of Mougi the ogre. He'd found us wandering in the dark of Everleaf Woods.

After Zeila's broom had been cut in half, all of her spells had weakened and failed, Mougi's mushroom patch included. While the mushrooms still tasted scrumptious and offered a huge variety of flavors, they no longer sent up poisonous clouds. Mougi was free to leave his patch.

The townsfolk of Tiller's Field met us at Mosswood Bridge. An enormous ogre is hard to miss, so they'd seen him coming. At first they were afraid but when they spotted us on the ogre's shoulders, a loud cheer went up. Any friend of the heroes of Tiller's Field was a friend of theirs, too.

Thankfully the townsfolk were people again, not frogs. Jozlyn had cried at seeing them, and even I'd felt a sticky lump in my throat.

We really had done it. The town was safe and Zeila was powerless without her broom. I thought we'd seen the last of her.

Everyone applauded us, hugged us, and patted us on the back. "Hip-hip-huzzah!" they shouted over and over as we walked quietly with our parents toward home. It was like a parade with us in the lead.

That night Dad had to send away dozens of visitors. Connor had been one of the first and most eager to see us. When Dad politely asked him to come back the next day, Connor agreed but not before sticking his head in the front door and shouting, "Not bad for peasants! Welcome home!"

The next morning a group of important visitors arrived. They stood outside the way they had on Cauldron Cooker's Night. Among them were Mayor Garlo in his crooked top hat, Wizard Ast, and Sheriff Logan looking as grim as ever.

Behind them stood Cleogha the witch. She looked quite different, and I almost didn't recognize her. She'd brushed her hair and put on a yellow outfit with pink trim.

"My, my," Mayor Garlo told us, puffing his bushy mustache with a big breath. "You have done quite well for yourselves. All of Tiller's Field thanks you and is in your debt." He paused and cleared his throat.

Wizard Ast leaned on his staff. "What the mayor is trying to tell you-say," he smiled through his beard, "is we wish to reward-repay you." He turned and nodded to Cleogha.

The yellow-dressed witch shuffled forward and extended her hand to Jozlyn. "This be yours," she said softly. "It be right that you have her back."

In the witch's hand was Rosie the pixie doll, looking as good as new. She didn't have a single rip or tear or spot of dirt.

Jozlyn cried out in joy. "Oh, Rosie!" she exclaimed, hugging the doll fiercely to her chest.

Mayor Garlo cleared his throat again. "We have decided that Witch Cleogha is no threat to out town and have agreed that she shall be allowed to return home. My, my. She may even fly on her broom on Cauldron Cooker's Night … so long as she is quiet about it."

"Furthermore," Wizard Ast added, "we have decided-determined that you two children are ready to begin-start training for your future."

Ast turned to Jozlyn. "You are hereby apprenticed to Witch Cleogha. You will learn-study the secrets of magic. Your skill-talent with the wand has demonstrated your aptitude."

Jozlyn gasped and her eyes went wide. I couldn't tell if she was excited about the idea of learning magic or worried about spending time with Cleogha.

The old wizard then turned to me. "You, lad, will be apprenticed to Sheriff Logan. Please kneel."

As stunned as Jozlyn, I numbly did what the wizard asked. I couldn't refuse with all of them standing there. But why did Sheriff Logan have to be involved? He scared me!

The sheriff's arm blurred and he drew his long sword in a single smooth motion. He rested the blade lightly upon my shoulder.

In a quiet but commanding voice, he said, "I dub thee Deputy Josh, my page. By courage and valor have you earned this honor." He lifted the sword and then touched my other shoulder with it. "Continue to serve Tiller's Field and I will see that you become a swordsman of legend. Now rise."

I stood up and Sheriff Logan held out his hand for me to shake. He had a big smile on his face, the first I'd ever seen there. Seeing it made me feel better about him, and I wasn't afraid of him anymore.

The four visitors left shortly after that. Our training would begin soon, but not immediately.

Jozlyn and I took a walk to Mosswood Bridge where we dangled our feet over the edge in the warm water. We were quiet for a while before Jozlyn finally spoke.

"Adventures never really end, do they Josh?" she asked while staring at the gurgling creek.

I thought about that a bit and decided she was right. We'd defeated Zeila in one adventure, but new adventures waited for us both.

"Not for heroes like us," I grinned. "Ribbit."

The End

The Knightscares Adventure Continues ...

#2: Skull in the Birdcage

#3: Early Winter's Orb

Knightscares #2:
Skull in the Birdcage

Special Preview

1

As soon as my eyes opened, I jumped out of bed. *Today's the day!* I excitedly reminded myself, as if I needed reminding. There wasn't anything that could make me forget.

Yawning, I shook my head, trying to clear it. I'd been too excited to sleep last night and I was paying for it. But there was no way I would let sleepiness slow me down.

I'd turned twelve the week before. That's the age a kid can become a knight. Well, a page really, which is another name for knight-in-training or a knight-to-be.

While I've always considered myself a knight, I was about to officially begin training.

I already knew how to ride a horse, carry a lance, and wield a sword. But a knight's training is more than practicing to fight. It's about learning the *Noble Deeds and Duties*. That's every knight's code of behavior. Aside from being strong, brave, and good in battle, a knight must know about honor and justice.

Act five of the *Noble Deeds and Duties* sums it up:

The Common Good Is Best Served by Uncommon Honor.

In other words, a knight must be honorable at all times for the good of everyone. As for the Acts, they're sort of the rules for knighthood. There are one hundred Acts in the *Noble Deeds and Duties*. I've been studying them for as long as I can remember.

I dressed quickly in my best outfit, a dark blue doublet trimmed in black, some blue hose, and a pair of low boots. Checking myself in the mirror, I thought I looked pretty knightly.

My blond hair was cut very short. Most knights wear their hair that way because it gets very hot under their helmets. I also thought I looked taller than I had the day before. Maybe I'd had another growth spurt during the night.

"Connor," my father liked to tease me, "stop growing so fast or we'll have to keep you in a barn." He was joking, of course. I wasn't *that* big. Besides, we didn't have a barn.

Following the delicious scent of bacon into the kitchen, I found that my parents had made breakfast for me. They'd left before the sun had risen to prepare for the Turning of the Pages ceremony.

That's where I needed to be by noon. The ceremony was where and when new pages were named. It happened only once a year and was a very big deal. Knights and pages from all over the kingdom would participate, not just people from Tiller's Field where I lived.

A soft knock on the front door told me that Simon had arrived. Simon was my age and was also going to be named a page. Only, unlike me, he didn't want to be.

Simon was kind of small, pretty clumsy, and more interested in books and magic tricks than swords and noble deeds. But his father was a knight just like mine, so Simon didn't have much choice.

I hauled the door open fast to startle him. "Good morning, peasant," I shouted to add to the surprise. I call everyone who isn't a knight "peasant". That included people like Simon who didn't want to be knights.

The *whoosh* of the door along with my loud voice worked perfectly. Simon sputtered in surprise and fumbled the four apples he'd been juggling. One even bounced off his head of floppy red hair.

Juggling was just about the only thing Simon could do that required coordination. As long as he wasn't distracted, that is.

"Good morning," Simon said cheerfully. Nothing much bothered him. Not even an apple bouncing on his head.

"Good morning, *sir*," I corrected. Peasants were supposed to call knights "sir".

Simon shrugged and rolled his eyes. "Whatever you say, *Sir* Bigmouth," he snickered. When I didn't laugh with him, he shrugged again, then scooped up his fallen apples.

No, Simon would never be a real knight. But he was a good sport.

Crrrrrunch. He bit into one of his apples.

"Got anything to eat?" he asked with a mouthful of fruit.

Got anything to eat, sir? I thought to myself. But there was no point in saying it out loud. Simon wouldn't change.

I never would have guessed it then, but I'm alive today because of Simon. A whole lot of people are. He's something of a hero. Brave and chivalrous just like a real knight. There's a lot more to him than you might expect from a clumsy bookworm.

2

Even though my parents had left breakfast for me, Simon ate most of it. I don't know where he put it all. He wasn't a very big kid.

If I ate like he did, I really would have to live in a barn!

After breakfast, we washed our dishes and left. The Turning of the Pages ceremony would take place outside of town at Battledown Yard. That's also where knights held jousting tournaments. The Yard was a couple of hours east of Tiller's Field, so we would have to hurry to be there by noon.

Lucky for us I had my own horse, Honormark, a spirited charger. I named him Honormark because of a black mark on his nose that looked like a shield. The rest of his body was white.

The stables were located on the other side of town. On

our walk, I decided to question Simon about something that had been bothering me.

"Why don't you want to be a knight?" I asked. "Are you happy being a peasant?"

Simon laughed and raised one eyebrow at me. I couldn't do that. Raise just one eyebrow. "You don't really believe all that peasant nonsense, do you?" he asked.

His question made me frown. "Sure I do," I said defensively. "There's royalty, knights, and peasants. In that order. Kings and queens are royalty and they're born that way. So that leaves knights or peasants for the rest of us."

He laughed again. "Can knights or peasants do this?"

With a quick flick of his wrist, he tossed an apple high above his head. It was exactly the same color as his hair. He juggled apples all the time, so I wasn't too impressed.

As the apple fell, he brought up his hands and mumbled something I didn't quite hear. The apple stopped falling and rotated slowly in mid-air.

"How did—?" I started to ask. Then Simon hooked his finger at the apple, and it shot through the air and bonked me on the head.

"That's for surprising me when you opened the door," Simon smirked, holding out his hand for me to shake. "Now we're even. Still friends?"

I shook his hand, laughing. I'd deserved getting hit with the apple. It was only fair for what I'd done to him earlier.

As for making the apple float in the air, almost anyone could learn magic tricks. Simon practiced them all the time. It's not like he was a wizard using real magic.

We arrived at the stables a short while later. Mr. Sootbeard the blacksmith has a big barn on his property where most everyone from Tiller's Field keeps their horses.

We called out for Mr. Sootbeard, but he didn't seem to be around. He wasn't in his house or in the forge out back. Usually there was smoke coming from the chimney and the clanging of a hammer coming from the forge.

"Maybe he's running an errand," Simon suggested.

"Could be," I agreed half-heartedly, but I knew Mr. Sootbeard better. He wouldn't leave without posting a sign or note. He had the only key to the stable.

Simon pointed at the stable. "Someone's inside," he whispered.

The stable door was slightly ajar. That meant that either Mr. Sootbeard was inside or that someone had broken in. Mr. Sootbeard wouldn't leave without locking up.

"Keep quiet and stay down," I said, crouching down and waving my arm for Simon to follow. We had to find out what was going on. It was the knightly thing to do.

We quietly crept across the yard to the stable and stopped to catch our breath. Pressed up against the wall next to the door, I took a deep gulp then silently mouthed the words, "One…two…three."

On *three*, I threw the door open wide and charged inside.

The interior of the stable was dark and strangely quiet. A short row of railed stalls formed a hallway that turned to the right a short distance ahead. The stalls were full of shadows and looked abandoned.

I stopped when I noticed that the gate to the stall on my left was open. Simon bumped into my back.

"Excuse..." he started to apologize, but I waved him off. There was something moving in the stall. Not a horse or Mr. Sootbeard. Something else. Something taller than my waist and covered with dark hair.

An angry growl came from the stall and yellow eyes stared out at me from the darkness.

3

"Heel, Thorn!" I called urgently, my voice cracking in panic.

Thorn was Mr. Sootbeard's dog, a baron mastiff that guarded his property. The dog was all teeth, muscles, and mean personality. But I couldn't understand why it was lurking in an empty stall.

The mastiff's growl was low and deep as it stalked slowly from the stall. The hackles on its neck stood up straight and its lips curled back in a snarl. Its yellow teeth were as thick as my thumb.

"*Thorn,*" I tried more calmly.

Thorn barked in warning. The familiarity of my voice wasn't having an effect. At least not a good one. I was going to have to defend myself.

A shovel used to clean the stables leaned against the wall

next to me. Without taking my eyes from Thorn's, I slowly reached out and grasped its handle.

Thorn dipped his big head and growled deeper, preparing for a fight.

I drew the shovel in front of me and gripped it like a staff in both hands. My mouth went suddenly dry and my heart pounded in my ears like a war drum. I didn't want to hurt Thorn, but the mastiff didn't seem to have any doubts about hurting me or Simon.

As he barked again, I raised the shovel.

"Wait!" Simon gasped from behind me. *"Bravery Without Honor Is Cowardice,"* he quoted from the *Noble Deeds and Duties*. It was Act Eleven. One I could never really figure out.

How could being brave make someone a coward?

Before I had time to wonder about what it meant, Simon stepped around me and knelt in front of Thorn. He stretched out a shaking hand toward the mastiff's nose and vicious teeth.

Thorn stopped advancing but kept growling. Drool dripped from his jaws.

"Thorrrnnn," Simon purred soothingly. His hand lightly touched the dog's quivering muzzle. "Down, boy. Sit."

Thorn's yellow eyes stared at Simon, and for a brief second, I got a sense that Thorn wanted nothing more than to sink his teeth into Simon's hand. But instead, the mastiff

196

whimpered quietly and dropped onto its stomach.

I sighed in relief and heard Simon do the same. He gently scratched Thorn's broad head.

"Something frightened him," he said thoughtfully. "He wouldn't normally threaten us, right?"

I shook my head vigorously. "No, never. He knows me. He's only supposed to act that way when danger is near."

Simon leaped to his feet. His face was white with fear. "Something's in here," he breathed quietly. "Something that scares Thorn."

Nodding, I clutched the shovel more tightly. Simon was right. Thorn was afraid of something.

I inched past Thorn and tried to control my breathing. My mouth was still dry but my hands were sweating. Fear has a way of turning everything upside down. For some reason, I was panting like I'd just run up a steep hill. My arms and legs felt all wobbly and weak. Simon breathed heavily behind me.

I knew that whatever could scare Thorn would be terrifying to us.

The Test of True Bravery Is to Embrace Fear, I told myself. Act Twenty-three. It meant that only when a knight is genuinely afraid can actions be considered brave. There is nothing heroic about doing something that doesn't make a person at least a little bit frightened.

I repeated the Act silently as we crept down the passage.

Straw and dirt crunched under our boots, and our heavy breathing echoed in the narrow corridor. Whatever waited ahead would surely hear us coming.

Just as we were about to turn the corner, someone shouted a loud "*Yah!*" from farther back in the stable. It was a scratchy voice like a person with a really bad sore throat.

"Look out!" I yelled, throwing myself into Simon. We crashed into a gate and tumbled into the stall just in the nick of time.

Honormark, my horse, charged around the corner at a gallop. His eyes were wide and his nostrils flared. On his back crouched an unshaven man wearing a long, blood-red cape.

They raced past us without a glance. If we hadn't fallen into the stall, we would have been trampled.

I was back on my feet in a rush, charging after Honormark and the thief-of-a-rider.

"Come back here," I demanded. "That's my horse!"

The scruffy rider burst through the stable door and pulled up Honormark's reins. In the sunlight outside I saw that he had squinty eyes and a big, hooked nose like a bird's beak. He wore a double-bladed axe strapped to his back and a dull black breastplate.

When I caught up to him, I pointed at Honormark. "That's my horse," I gasped, out of breath. I was too angry to be afraid.

The man sneered at me and laughed. "King's business, peasant," he rasped at me.

"Peasant?" I blurted furiously. This man didn't know that he was talking to a knight!

He threw back his cape and pointed at the insignia on his left shoulder. It was the king's crest, a red rose draped over a golden crown. Only the highest-ranking knights wore that symbol.

The thief must be one of the king's personal knights.

My jaw dropped and the man laughed at me again. With a vicious kick, he spurred Honormark into a trot. "The king thanks you for your generosity, peasant," the thieving knight called arrogantly over his shoulder.

Then he was gone in a cloud of dust from under Honormark's hooves.

4

I hate feeling helpless.

Knights are supposed to be strong and able to defend themselves. But I hadn't been able to stop the scruffy-looking knight from stealing my horse. To him I was just some dopey kid. A nobody.

A peasant.

I threw my arms up in frustration and stared in the direction Honormark and the rider had gone. Toward the eastern side of town. It was the same way Simon and I needed to go to reach the Turning of the Pages ceremony.

"Let's find Sheriff Logan," Simon suggested. Deep in my thoughts, I'd almost forgotten Simon was there.

I turned sharply on my heels. Normally I would go straight to the sheriff to report a crime. It's his job to track down criminals.

Only today I had somewhere extremely important to be. I couldn't afford to spend the time it would take to find the sheriff and explain what had happened. If Simon and I wanted to reach Battledown Yard by noon, we'd have to hurry.

I grabbed Simon by the sleeve and turned him toward the stable. "Come on," I told him, "we have to find another horse or we won't make it in time."

"But that's stealing!" Simon protested. "Act Five—*Use Only That Which Is Earned or Freely Given.*"

For someone who didn't want to be a knight, he sure knew a lot about the *Noble Deeds and Duties.*

"Well, it would be," I explained, "if we were really going to steal a horse. But we aren't. We're going to borrow one."

Simon started to object but I cut him off. I knew he wanted to remind me that borrowing without permission was almost as bad as stealing. But he didn't know that I had permission to borrow this horse.

Last summer, my friends Josh and Jozlyn had rescued our town after everyone had been turned into frogs. Afterward, they'd been rewarded. Josh became Sheriff Logan's deputy and Jozlyn was named apprentice to a good witch.

Jozlyn is very busy learning about magic. As a favor, she'd asked me to exercise her old horse Zippity. So whenever I visited Honormark, I took Zippity for a little ride, too.

Today I'd take Zippity for a longer ride, that's all.

I quickly explained this to Simon. He seemed unsure but decided to go along with me. He didn't want to walk all the way to Battledown Yard any more than I did. Riding would take long enough.

We found Zippity in her stall munching lazily on some hay. She was a chubby, brown mare with white socks. Calling her Zippity was kind of funny. Zipping usually means moving fast, but Zippity was anything but fast. I think she thought of herself as a cow instead of a horse.

Even with both of us riding her, we quickly left the town behind and followed Wagonwheel Road toward the jousting yard. A glance overhead told me that we had two hours before the ceremony started. Just enough time if we hurried.

I started to get excited again and forgot about the scruffy knight who'd stolen Honormark. Simon and I were going to become knights today. Everything else would turn out all right.

Riding behind me, Simon broke our silence. "Bring anything to eat?" he asked.

I almost fell out of the saddle. How could he be hungry again? "You can't be serious!" I exclaimed. "We just had breakfast."

Simon fidgeted. "Well…maybe a snack. We've got a big

day ahead."

"But you don't even want to be a knight," I replied.

"Maybe not for my whole life," he admitted, "but while I am, I'm going to try as hard as I can. And to do that, I need a full stomach!" He chuckled and shoved my back playfully.

We both laughed at that, and I thought about what he'd said as we rode. His words made me think of Act Eighteen.

In All Things, Both Noble and Common, Strive Toward Excellence.

Simon might not want to be a knight, but he still planned on being a good one.

That attitude can help out in lots of places. In school, work, and even chores. I know when I try my best at something, I usually don't have to do it twice.

When the sun was almost overhead, we reached Battledown Yard. Knights, horses, and soon-to-be pages crowded the long, grassy field. Flags bearing the king's colors waved from tall poles. Banners depicting scenes of famous battles hung from the large grandstand where the real knights and spectators sat.

I spotted my father and waved, but I don't think he saw me. He was reading from a long scroll and frowning.

Simon and I tethered Zippity and then hurried to find a

seat on the grass in front of the grandstand. We sat on the track where the jousting competitions took place.

Normally an audience would watch from the grandstand but not today. Today, dozens of kids crowded around us on the grass waiting excitedly to be named pages.

"This is it," I beamed at Simon. I was so excited that I couldn't keep from smiling.

Simon nodded and swallowed. He looked nervous. "Sure is," he said quietly.

The Turning of the Pages began with a blowing of trumpets. When their great blare sounded, people all around us cheered and whooped for several minutes. I cheered right along with them. Simon hardly breathed.

The noise died down when two older pages on the grandstand stepped forward. They carried polished lances with flags tied to their tips, and waved them back and forth. The trumpets blared again.

A group of knights in polished armor came forward next. My father was one of them. The group stopped at the edge of the grandstand and my father looked over the field.

"Today," he told us in his deep voice, "is the day you have waited for."

The crowd erupted in more cheering, whistling, and clapping.

My father raised his hands to ask for silence. "But it is my sad duty to inform you…." He cleared his throat and glanced at someone behind him. "It is my sad duty to inform you that there will be no ceremony today."

A gasp went through the crowd. Then there was a heavy silence.

"Please welcome Sir Filabard, Knight of the King's Right Hand," my father announced, turning to the man behind him. "He will explain the reason for today's cancellation."

I gasped again when Sir Filabard brushed past my father to address the crowd. I recognized his bird-like nose and scruffy face.

Sir Filabard was the man who'd stolen my horse.

End of the Preview

Knightscares #2:
Skull in the Birdcage

Available now!

Ask for it at your bookstore or order online at
www.knightscares.com

Want Free Knightscares?

Join the Free Knightscares Fan Club Today!

www.knightscares.com

*Get the latest news and info on Knightscares
from the co-wizards, David and Charlie.*

Join the Fan Club
Get Your Name on the Knightscares Website
Preview Upcoming Adventures
Invite the Authors to Your School
Meet the Writers
Lots More!

Knightscares
Drawing Contest

Like to draw?

Send your drawings to Knightscares for a chance to win a free autographed book. Your picture might just be chosen to appear in a future Knightscares adventure. Check out www.knightscares.com for more info.

Send Your Drawings to:
Knightscares Artwork
P.O. Box 654
Union Lake, MI   48387

Cauldron Cooker's Night Artwork

The hand-painted cover art, official Knightscares logo, maps, and interior illustrations were all created by the talented artist Steven Spenser Ledford.

Steven is a free-lance fine and graphic artist from Charleston, SC with nearly 20 years experience. His work includes public and private wall murals, comic book pencil, ink and color, magazine illustrations and cover art, t-shirt designs, sculptures, portraits, painted furniture and more. Most of his work is produced from the tiny rooms of the house he shares with his very patient wife and their two children—Xena (a psychotic tortoise-shell cat) and Emma (a Jack Russell terrier). He welcomes inquiries at PtByNmbrs@aol.com.

Thank you, Steven!